"Don't!" Wrenn yelled. "He's part of a case I'm working! He knows something about—!"

"No vampires in Oberon's Castle!" Robin interrupted. "You sent in pictures, Wrenn."

"But—"

The ball of magic elongated into a spike. Robin pulled back his arm. And that spike pierced the kelpie's vampire heart.

Light magic blazed. Dark magic roiled. The kelpie-vampire turned into a suffocating dust cloud....

DEATH KISSED

NORTHERN CREATURES BOOK SIX

KRIS AUSTEN RADCLIFFE

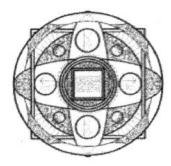

THE WORLDS OF
KRIS AUSTEN RADCLIFFE

Smart Urban Fantasy:

Northern Creatures

Monster Born

Vampire Cursed

Elf Raised

Wolf Hunted

Fae Touched

Death Kissed

God Forsaken

Magic Scorned

Witch Burned (*coming soon*)

Genre-bending Science Fiction about
love, family, and dragons:

WORLD ON FIRE

Series one

Fate Fire Shifter Dragon

Games of Fate

Flux of Skin

Fifth of Blood

Bonds Broken & Silent

All But Human

Men and Beasts

The Burning World

Dragon's Fate and Other Stories

Series Two

Witch of the Midnight Blade

Witch of the Midnight Blade Part One

Witch of the Midnight Blade Part Two

Witch of the Midnight Blade Part Three

Witch of the Midnight Blade: The Complete Series

Series Three

World on Fire

Call of the Dragonslayer (*coming soon*)

Hot Contemporary Romance:

The Quidell Brothers

Thomas's Muse

Daniel's Fire

Robert's Soul

Thomas's Need

Quidell Brothers Box Set

Includes:

Thomas's Muse

Daniel's Fire

Roberts's Soul

DEATH KISSED

NORTHERN CREATURES
Book Six

By
Kris Austen Radcliffe

Six Talon Sign Fantasy & Futuristic Romance
Minneapolis

www.krisaustenradcliffe.com

First print edition, July 2020
Version: 10.19.2022

ISBN: 978-1-939730-76-3

DEATH KISSED

CHAPTER 1

Oberon's Castle, the Fae Realms...

Malfeasance is a sticky syrup that took effort to create—one had to boil down one's narcissistic tendencies just right to get that perfect gooey consistency for smothering the life out of the world. And there was always someone—mundane or magical—who lived for the perverse satisfaction of brewing up the worst of the universe. They didn't care who suffered.

What caught Wrenn Goodfellow off guard was the number of knives-out sous chefs ready to do the villain's chopping and slicing.

Wrenn peered at the magic dancing along the edge of the bayberry-scented, semi-translucent vellum she held. Such sheets were milled from the scales shed by butterfly-winged pixies, the self-right-eous kind who supposedly never lied, and were hard to come by. They were renowned for their clarity of "truth and magic."

In Oberon's Castle, "truth" keyed itself to its holder and more often than not, "magic" was the lock imprisoning what was real.

Such slipperiness made whipping up a vast kettle of malice all that much easier.

Wrenn rotated the vellum slightly to better catch the last golden shine of the sunset flowing across the threshold between her sunroom and kitchen. She adjusted the angle slightly to keep the sheet perpendicular to her line of sight, and watched the eddies and vortices of aurora-like blues, purples, and greens as they swirled and flowed over the data spells attached to the sheet.

That shine was why she spent a significant portion of her monthly Royal Guard salary on her small but comfortable apartment. Why she'd fought to get a west-facing place in one of the calmer premium realms. Her aquariums did well here—her fish plinked and gurgled in the sunroom—as did her rainforest's worth of potted plants.

Those huge windows on the other side of the arched threshold, those sheets of glass made by fae artisans, acted as a megaphone.

And there, along the edge of the vellum, a little bit of truth surfaced out of the dancing magic: A tiny ballerina manifested on the corner. She danced to one side, then back, like a looped video.

Wrenn had no idea what the ballerina itself meant. Did the dead sprite identified on the clarity-laden vellum moonlight as a dancer in the mundane world? Did she dance here, for one of the Royal Courts? Or had dancing been her dream?

Charmed artifacts like pixie vellum tended to be well cared for and used again and again. Wrenn had managed to get this one before the report was transferred into Oberon's new digital archive and the paper sent to be used for a more important case.

She rotated it again to get a good look at the overwritten magic under the report, just in case something leaked through and corrupted the information.

The clarity of that dancing ballerina said it wasn't a corruption. Whoever made this report cared enough to take the extra steps necessary to restrain older magic from seeping up into the details of this particular murder.

Some officer had decided he needed to write up his report on the special lie-detector paper. Not, she suspected, because at the time he thought the eyewitness account all that important, but because he thought the witness was lying.

Every cop knew that sprites were "like that" when they thought they could get something from a lie, like ruining the reputation of a good and charitable fae lord. Because when was every cop wrong?

Then the sprite washed up dead on the banks of the Titan River three realms distant from the good and charitable fae lord's lands, her ethereal gossamer wings chewed down to her back and her body drained of blood.

Such murders were a dime a dozen in the fae realms that made up Oberon's Castle. Every magical group had their malevolent entities. The kami had their evil yōkai, and the elves had their Loki aspects. But the fae had entire breeds who specialized in terrorizing not only mundanes, but also other fae—ogres who ate children, kelpie who stalked and murdered women, boggarts who were snot-eating cowards who harassed strangers on both the mundane and fae internets. Plus at least fifteen other types of fae whose entire reason for being was maliciousness.

So no one in Oberon's Royal Guard even batted a sweet eyelash when the sprite washed onto the shore hacked up and exsanguinated.

Wrenn did, though.

The sprite had made the harassment report detailed on the vellum a year—almost to the exact date—before she washed up. There was nothing particularly magically special about the number of days, or weeks, or hours for that matter, so the investigators chalked it up to chance.

Wrenn set the vellum on top of the pile of case files spread out across her kitchen table. Magic wafted off the report in waves and tightly woven curlicues. No jagged breaks or unharmonious colors distorted the account.

The witness definitely had believed what she reported.

The sprite's big-eyed photo shimmered on the top left of the sheet. Next to it, her name and home realm. Under that, a sigil that unlocked a spell replaying the sprite's interview.

Wrenn's inherent magic was neither intricate nor powerful enough to replay a record spell, so she tapped her paladin star to call up a replay token. The star—a rosy, seven-pointed shield made of a lovely champagne-colored fae silver-and-gold steel—was standard issue for the Royal Guard. Like most law officers' identification, it was about the size of her palm.

As an official Paladin to the King—the Royal Guard equivalent to a mundane detective—she never pinned it onto her jacket but instead carried it in a flip wallet much like mundane FBI agents. Her star had an enchanted clip that would hold it to her belt no matter what hits she took.

Wrenn's star also carried the enchantment tokens issued to her by the Royal Guard.

She absently ran her finger over the surface of the star to pick up an unlock spell, then touched it to the vellum's written documentation to bring up the transcript of the sprite's complaint.

There'd been a party—there were always parties, with the fae lords —and the sprite had been employed to serve wine and mead. Drunkenness happened. Unsurprising gropings occurred. The fae were not particularly modern in their understanding of consent or bodily autonomy, and boundaries had not been respected.

Again, Wrenn was not surprised. She continued to read.

And there, buried deep in the debauchery, the words for which she'd been hunting: *There were...* (witness pauses) *I don't remember,* witness says.

Sprites remembered everything. *Not* remembering suggested an enthralling.

I feel so tired.... (pauses again)

The sprite had been pale when the Guard arrived that night.

I don't think they were fae.

Wrenn tapped her kitchen table and sat back in her chair.

Two hundred years in Oberon's Castle had taught her one thing: Dark magicals would work together if a sufficient nexus of power pulled them into its orbit. A nexus such as a powerful vampire.

Only a handful of Guard knew the truth: No magical was more cancerous than a vampire—so cancerous that their presence inflicted damage on the realms. When the black void of death magic that was the demon at the heart of a vampire corrupted enough, it changed a realm physically, structurally, and magically.

4

A strong enough vampiric presence would destroy a realm if left unchecked, literally breaking down the spellwork that held the realm in place.

So Wrenn watched the Eastern European vampires for signs of organization, something that signaled the rise of power among their kind. She watched the Japanese vampires for the same reason, though most of those vamps were born from a different process than their European counterparts, and did not tolerate outsiders. She watched the American Gulf Coast clans, and consumed every scrap of information she could about the North American elves who, for some bizarre reason, were harboring low-powered vamps. She kept tabs on the Peruvian vampire hives. She knew of small gatherings in several African nations, and of one or two in Australia and New Zealand.

Even though her personal magic was close to nonexistent, she was the King's best vampire hunter. Keeping vampires out of Oberon's Castle, and out of all fae business both Seelie and Unseelie, light and dark, inside the realms and out-, was why she held Paladin status within the Royal Guard.

The dead sprite was the eleventh incident in the last month.

Exsanguination. Often mutilation. Always a low-powered magical whose blood would at least give a vampire a high, and at most act like super-soldier serum.

And now the King had vampires *inside* his Castle. At least one of the bloodsuckers had found a way to get across one of the many veils between the mundane world and the fae realms.

Which meant a dark magical somewhere figured the central realms under the King's control were robust enough to invite a vampire into the house.

Probably. She had no actual proof that a vampire had gotten into Oberon's Castle. The sprite could have been trafficked into the mundane world and then dumped here.

Still, operating directly under the King's nose would not bode well for any vampire or hive. Unless something big had happened, disrupting the power hierarchies among *all* the vampires, and they were out of control.

She had no idea what, or how, or where, which strongly suggested the involvement of other magicals. Powerful ones capable of hiding their tracks.

And there was another truth here. One the Royal Guard needed to deal with now.

The fae had a blood trafficking syndicate on their hands. A syndicate that, until recently, had been operating on a low enough level that it had been able to hide. Or the King didn't care.

Wrenn rubbed her forehead and looked out over the table at the golden evening light streaming through the doorway into her sunroom. She was pretty sure *this* vampire issue was about to merge with her *other* vampire issue. The personal one. And that the King would think she was blowing the whole thing out of proportion because of her past.

But her gut told her that what had likely been considered a "minor" dark fae problem in the eyes of the royals was about to blossom into an all-out war.

If only Oberon would believe she wasn't chasing her own ghosts.

Wrenn swiped a transfer spell off her star and used it to pick up the list of known contacts for the dead sprite. She tapped her phone's screen and the list transferred to her official Royal Guard app.

She tucked the vellum sheet into its protective sleeve and picked up her mug, carefully curling her aching hands around the blue water pattern along its outside. Ignoring her background pain was easier with her mind on the files, but the warmth moving from the mug into the death-like chill encompassing her fingers shifted her attention to her joints.

The chill danced on her skin and hardened her muscles when she slept. It stiffened her limbs and made moving difficult until she'd exercised enough to warm up.

But today—Samhain—was special. There was something about the Eight Festivals in a fae realm that shifted her basal metabolic rate. Beltane brought too much heat to her bones. Samhain caused the cold aches to ride her muscles into the evening.

Reviewing case files meant lighter work for the day, which she needed, since she couldn't whip up a relief spell. Not until dawn tomorrow morning, when Samhain ended.

She was a witch living in Oberon's Castle. Witches were forbidden to use magic during any of the Eight Festivals, and today was the most magical of all. The veil between realms was at its thinnest tonight, and witches weren't good at magic, so they were to stay quiet and leave the spells to the good full-breed fae who were capable of controlling all those vivid interactions.

So Wrenn Goodfellow, the Fae King's investigative paladin and witch of unknown heritage, closed her eyes and once more did her best to will away the pain, which she knew wouldn't work. But at least it allowed her to pretend it sent away the army of nerve goblins chewing on her muscles.

For a split second, she had a vision of a parade of tiny literal goblins, all about the size of her fingertips, sitting along the arch of her thumb where she held her mug of tea. One wrinkled his wee puke-green nose and nodded toward her. *Hey baby, how ya doin'?* he screeched. The two on either side of him grabbed their crotches.

Wrenn pinched her eyes closed. Damned fae Samhain twisting her ability to see magic. She never had these problems when she spent the holiday in the mundane world.

She sipped her tea. The work called, anyway.

The next file was surveillance on a kelpie under suspicion of moving in and out of the mundane world more than he was legally allowed. His regular evil kelpie behavior wasn't the problem. Someone was keeping an eye on him because he was basically jumping the turnstiles and misusing the fae realms' public transportation system to move in and out of real-world cities.

Seemed also he'd dappered himself up all nice and clean and started a Nazi-lite group of women-haters. An extraordinarily *wealthy* group, and all that gold wasn't coming from his group's social media grifts, either.

And he'd figured out how to move between the fae realms and the real world with impunity.

This kelpie was likely trafficking for someone powerful.

Wrenn looked up at the ceiling of her small kitchen. She needed to remember that the kelpie might not be part of their vampire problem. His nexus of power could be any dark magical. Some nasty elf, or even a malicious nine-tailed kitsune looking to expand outside of Japan.

But there was a chance.

Likely suspects would be out tonight, popping in and out of Oberon's Castle as they took advantage of Samhain's thinning veils, partying and visible and accessible. So would every sprite and house fae on the list she'd lifted off the vellum sheet.

Some she could bring in. Most, not. On the streets, the power and word of a paladin only carried so much weight. But she was not to be out tonight. Not being a—

She glanced back at the threshold into her sunroom. Accidentally, and without thinking about the sunset, or the light, or possible triggered vivid thoughts. She'd let her mind wander with her work and now...

Now she paid the price.

CHAPTER 2

I t'd been six years since she'd had a flashback. Six years of thinking that maybe, just *maybe*, the out-of-nowhere memory intrusions had finally stopped. That after over two hundred years of living with the fae she'd finally found some semblance of peace.

Wrenn had stupidly thought she could look at case files involving dark fae—no, *vampires*—and that all she'd have to deal with was a little extra pain because she wasn't allowed to cast relief spells for the next twenty-four hours.

But it was Samhain, and her ability to see magic—no matter how unique and coveted by Oberon it might be—made her vulnerable.

The Samhain sunset hit the edge of her window and etched a line across the floor's stones. On one side of the boundary, shadow. On the other, extending from the window's arch into the kitchen, and to the side of her unadorned big toe, a harsh, icy-hot line of white light.

And an uncalled, unbidden memory sideswiped Wrenn's mind:

Blue light streamed off a metal rod so tall it poked up through the roof of the tenement. Blinding, bottled electricity arced from that rod to the racks of bottles and tools along the walls.

The little hairs on her forearms stood on end. She stood on end, too, drawn up onto her toes by the buzz roiling from the laboratory and into the living quarters.

She lived in the tenement with a man. Her captor. He mostly worked at night, under the moon, but this evening a storm raged.

And that rod...

The shrillness of the machinery had almost drowned out the driving rain pounding against the tenement. The building rocked. Thunder crashed. Lightning struck and the rod screamed with light so bright it turned the laboratory white.

Then an edge cut that light, too. A shadow slashed the cold blue touching her foot.

The monster shimmered with the blinding electrical buzz. The raw lightning bolt scar on the side of his face glowed. He rolled his massive shoulders and he roared at the storm outside.

In his laboratory, under the blistering blue light, her captor had stitched arms to a chest. He'd implanted a heart meant to pump a monster's blood through its stolen veins. He'd added legs. A head.

Fangs.

Her captor stood two paces from his creation and for some reason, for some prickly numbness, she remembered the dark, blotchy stain on the arm of his otherwise perfectly white shirt. He liked his clothing pristine. He always smiled and thanked her when she cleaned his shirts well. Told her that whiteness reminded him of his mother's loving touch and that she should be proud to be compared to such an excellent woman.

The monster clasped his massive hand around her captor's throat.

"Oh, Victor," she'd whispered. *You fool,* she'd thought.

This will be your final mistake.

Fear stiffened her bones. Horror quaked through her arms and legs. The monster was a vampire. He was a monster's monster, and all monsters were a threat.

To her, yes. But mostly to their makers.

The vampire sank his fangs into the side of Victor Frankenstein's neck.

One, she counted. *Two. Three,* and the white tone of Victor's skin changed from the ruddy physical manifestation of abject terror to the rubbery thickness of meat without blood.

The vampire lifted his head away like a swimmer coming up for air. And then he ripped Victor's skull from his body.

The memory changed: A flash of running through the storm. Of trees and wolves and deep wooded darkness.

Then Robin Goodfellow found her in the muddy forests outside Edinburgh.

Wrenn inhaled sharply. The exhale stuttered out of her throat as one popping whoosh. Two more quick breaths followed.

She wasn't in Victor's lab. Her feet touched the stone floor of her apartment.

And she stood up.

Stood so fast that she'd knocked her tea onto the files.

"Damn it!" Damaging the pixie vellum meant—

She dropped a towel onto the tea and the files. When had she picked up the towel?

Samhain, she thought. *Damn it damn it damn it.*

This wasn't the first time a thinning veil had caused a flashback. She should have realized one was coming.

She should have realized. She...

Wrenn extended her arm, her hand perpendicular to the floor. Her fingers shook. Her eyes blinked rapidly. Her breaths were too shallow, but she had the magic to get it under control, rules be as damned as her flashbacks.

She sighted along the shaft of bright pre-Samhain sunshine touching her toe. She inhaled again and mentally grabbed at the red and green magic floating around her body. A containment spell manifested at her fingertips.

She flicked it at the shadow's edge.

The flick was more symbolic than direct; the memory was inside her head, not on the floor. But the magic understood, and the magic did its work.

The tension caused by the flashback yanked out of the muscles of her head. The tightening around her eyes that distorted her vision and the spasming in her jaw that caused her to grind her teeth pulled away. Then the spell forced the tension down her neck and into the large muscles of her upper back.

She placed her hand on her stomach. The magic forced the knots in her belly into the large muscles of her backside and her legs.

The panic would wait there as potential energy, in storage, for as long as she needed.

"Why now?" she whispered. It'd been six years. *The monster's not here*, she thought. Not in Oberon's Castle, and most certainly not in her apartment.

Her investigations had not yet yielded any concrete information about the demon built by the fool named Victor Frankenstein. The monster had vanished after he killed Victor. No overt signs remained. No trail of corpses, or tales of an eight-foot demon. Nothing at all. She had only the artifacts and papers rescued from Victor's burned-out laboratory—a diary detailing his first attempt at his corpse-building alchemy. About how that monster had murdered Victor's younger brother.

And the monster's other travesties.

At least Victor had left her evidence that he'd killed the fiend on an Arctic ice floe.

She looked at the case files again. When she looked back at the threshold, the line between light and shadow distorted. The shadow buckled and the sun refracted around the door's frame.

A rainbow of color manifested for a fraction of a second. Only for that fraction—only that micro-moment—as the light transitioned across the edge.

"Heh," she said. If she believed in portents, she would have dropped to her knees and wailed.

"*He's* part of this, isn't he?" she asked the magic of Samhain.

He had to be. How, though, she didn't know.

On the floor, the edge of light moved away from her big toe. She inhaled yet again, and exhaled slowly, and a little voice at the back of her head said it was safe to look at the windows again.

She hated that little whispering inner voice. Hated that it was both her savior and her jailor.

Wrenn blinked a few times to clear any residual vividness. She faced the Samhain sunset. She'd go out. She'd find a concrete lead. Something that would let her take care of Victor Frankenstein's demon once and for all.

Time to do her job.

Time to hunt monsters.

CHAPTER 3

Outside Wrenn's windows, beautiful chrysanthemum fireworks blossomed in the sky in blues, greens, reds, and purples. Booms followed, and lots of laughter from the street.

She'd chosen this particular realm because it reminded her of the Edinburgh of her memories—cobbled streets and strong, solid timber-and-brick buildings, though the streets here were narrower and the buildings stretched taller. Rich oranges and savory browns warmed every corner and gave the borough an autumnal harvest/Samhain feel. The fae here preferred the thickness of velvet and brocades and tended to dress as if they were the true royalty of the realm.

And tonight, they would be out and glammed up to the fullest extent of their gloriousness.

Wrenn buckled the top closures on her black boots, then zipped her black leather jacket. The fae of Oberon's realms understood why a witch of unknown heritage had been allowed to live among them —her life with Victor Frankenstein had unlocked gifts of speed, strength, and stamina as well as her ability to see magic. She was also taller than most fae and mundanes alike, and remarkably durable.

When Robin had found her, he'd immediately recognized her potential, and Oberon had agreed.

It gave her a life in the Royal Guard, which in turn gave her training, access to a wealth of data for her searches, and worthwhile work.

Wrenn coiled her black hair into a knot and secured it with two sticks specially charmed to hold her thick, uncooperative locks up and out of her face. Like the rest of her body, her hair liked to stay ever-stalwart and unchanging, and would immediately return to its default cascade down her back the moment she set it free. Without access to fae hairdressers, she would have given up and shorn it off ages ago.

She fed her fish and placed her paladin star on her belt. Then she made her way into the Samhain celebrations gearing up all through Oberon's Castle.

Some of the royals slapped their names on every single blade of grass and pebble in their territory—Titania's Falls, for example, or the Titan River, which flowed through not just Titania's lands, but pretty much every fae realm.

Maybe the King was mad his wife had named the river after herself. Maybe he wanted to outdo the intricately manifested shadows of Tokyo and Osaka built by the kami. Or maybe he was mad that the fae could not live in the real world alongside their mundanes the way the elves did. So he compensated.

King Oberon controlled the fae metropolis called Oberon's Castle.

Goblins, brownies, pixies; gorgeous Seelie and terrifying Unseelie; changelings and every half-breed fae-born witch ever located by the Royal Guard—Oberon modernized his magicals and set them up adjacent to the mundane world in an interconnected, urbanized maze of interlocking realms.

Wrenn stepped across her building's threshold into air thick with sparking fae magic. Pixies drew curlicue trails at eye level. A moose-antlered Unseelie hunter danced in the street despite his kind's aversion to Oberon's urbanization. Sprites twirled in dresses as gossamer as their wings. Satyrs pranced. The Seelie paraded in processions. And above it all, fireworks blazed and boomed.

And this was just Wrenn's quiet, backwater home.

15

Tonight the world moved into the dark half of her year, the cold, dead part called winter. The entire planet crossed a threshold, and in doing so made all crossings easy. Anyone with enough fae blood could cross over into the mundane world with ease tonight if they so desired, and without paying a toll on the fae side.

Wrenn walked into the festivities. Crystalline laughter rose to her left. To her right, a tall, muscular male fae stripped off his shirt before lifting a smaller, curvy pink female into the air. A small band of drunken domestic hobgoblins, all carrying steins of sweet-smelling mead, sang out a well-harmonized chorus of "Ah great lady Queen, oh our divine comedy be seen," as they stumbled by.

Wrenn pulled out her phone and checked the contacts list she'd transferred from the pixie vellum. The murdered sprite had been from a realm called Applebottom, an adorable place of twinkling bluebells, fluffy clouds, and talking squirrels in pantaloons whose entire purpose was to turn the realm into a civilization sized for rodents, from root to crown of the realm's grand apple trees.

It also happened to be sized for sprites, and wasn't a place the six-foot-tall Wrenn should be stomping around after dark. Especially Samhain evening.

But there was another option.

If Wrenn wanted to find leads, she needed to head into the heart of Oberon's Castle—Oberon's actual castle. Lords and ladies would be about, and other high-powered fae, which meant she'd have access to their many servants.

And the odds of her finding a talkative sprite were much higher.

She did a mental check on the slight tingling along the Celtic tattoos circling both forearms just above her wrists like a pair of wide, intricate silver cuffs. The tattoos acted as anchors—wallets, really—for any non-work-related enchantments and tokens she wished to carry.

She might be a witch, but her magicks were limited and mostly protective. She could shield herself from a lot of what was tossed at her, be it magic or a punch. She couldn't enchant or enthrall, or even hit someone or something with much of a jolt.

So she had to buy enchantment tokens. Some were simple lidding magic she used so she didn't spill her coffee. Some were tracers for situations where she didn't want to use official enchantments from her star. But mostly they were tokens to pay for her Heartway use in a way that didn't open her soul.

Even though the Heartway was a public transportation system, it was still fae, and it demanded an exchange. Most fae paid with a little bit of their magicks. Some witches did, also. But Wrenn didn't want to deplete her inherent shielding magic any more than she wanted to allow the Heartway to take as it pleased from her psyche.

Letting others into her head—even if that other was a systemic magic and not a person—was not... comfortable. And after her little intrusive visitation from Victor earlier, the last thing she wanted tonight was to give the systemic magic of the fae more access to her deepest wounds.

She counted one tingle. One token. She had been planning on stopping yesterday on her way home but forgot when she got her hands on the case files spread out on her kitchen table. And now, this late and on Samhain evening, refilling her tattoos would be difficult.

Fireworks exploded down the street and the boom rolled through the air like a pressure front before a particularly strong spell manifested. It washed over her, wince-inducing and amplifying and crackling like electricity. The entire street brightened for a split second and all the ambient magic—all the wisps around the dancing sprites, all the aurora-like sheets trailing the Seelie parading through the streets —*howled*.

Wrenn pinched her eyes closed and reflectively grabbed her ears as the wave's crackle rolled by. She blinked and willed her eyes to focus through the blue-white haze left behind by the spell and—

Victor, she thought.

No more flashbacks! she yelled in her own head even though she knew better. She wasn't having a flashback. Not like the one she'd had in her kitchen. Victor wasn't here. Nor were his demons. She was on the street in the fae realm she called home. Fae partied all around her, happy and boisterous and full of glee.

This was not a place of obvious danger.

Yet her body braced for the possibility of the danger that welled up around her flashbacks. The loss of control. The semi-blackouts. The ragings and the screams.

She was terrifying to everyone around her when she flashed back, and she couldn't do that on the street. On Samhain. Why had she come out here in the first place?

Someone put a hand on her shoulder. "Wrenn?"

Wrenn whipped around.

Rich raised her hands. "You shouldn't be out here." She stood in front of Wrenn in the sturdy pants and black leather bustier over a spotless white blouse she always wore while tending bar. Behind her, a warm glow poured through the grand window of her tavern and framed Rich's semi-controlled blaze of red hair.

Rich and her partner Lush were both beautiful women—both red-haired, though Rich's hair was more red than orange—and both half-fae witches who often didn't get a lot of respect from the full fae in the area.

Rich shouldn't be out in the reverie any more than Wrenn.

Nor should Wrenn be standing in front of the tavern.

All the buildings in her neighborhood faced the same street. Turn a corner, and you were back on Main Street, just in a different area. The whole cross-section hatchwork of the magic had been confusing for about three decades until she'd figured out the underlying geometry.

Yet here she was.

Samhain clearly had decided to slap Wrenn across the face the moment she stepped outside. Why, though? The visions weren't a new manifestation with a festival, but they were coming faster and stronger than she'd expected when she'd decided to step out of her apartment.

Rich watched a Seelie couple stroll by. She blinked a few times as if being outside made her nervous. "Come in." She looked up and down the street, as if watching for the cops even though Wrenn was the local Royal Guard.

How had Wrenn gotten to the tavern? Was this a manifestation of her flashbacks, the same as when she found herself standing over her case files with a towel in her hand? Maybe Rich wasn't real, yet the perfect scent combination of roasting meats and warmed breads flowed out of the door. Wrenn inhaled deeply, centering herself.

Rich peered into her eyes. "Lush is having strong visions, too," she whispered. "We both are."

So it wasn't just Wrenn.

"You okay?" Rich touched Wrenn's arm.

Empathy was a commodity among the fae, and real caring was as rare and precious as gold. It was also more likely to happen among the witches.

Like Lush, Rich was a witch fathered by a fae and born to a mundane woman. Wrenn's height and strength fueled rumors that she was a witch with elf ancestry. She didn't know. No one knew, but the rumor did give some of the more annoying fae pause.

The magic around Rich flared outward from her like a roiling ball of reddish heat. She shuddered and blinked, then rubbed her forehead. The streetlamp flickered. The lights in the tavern brightened and buzzed. Rich looked up, frowned, and shifted how she held her shoulders.

The reddish magical heat around her danced up and into the air, and the lights went back to normal. "Sorry. Hot flash."

"S'okay," Wrenn said. The hot flash thing happened to all the witches in Oberon's Castle. Except for Wrenn. Not a lot of hot to flash when you woke up every morning with cold skin.

Rich chuckled. "Got to pay the rent somehow, huh?"

In the real world, that heat often caused the witch to overheat in mind and body. But in the connected realms of Oberon's Castle, a spellwork infrastructure siphoned off any flare-up before it hurt anyone.

Wrenn had long wondered where all that witch heat went. Still, without the siphoning, Rich and Lush would live vastly different lives, if they lived at all.

Rich waved her toward the door.

Some patrons played throwing games in the back. Some talked boisterously at the tables. All buzzed as they partied away the last of the year's light before winter officially hit.

Wrenn followed Rich through the crowd and sat at the bar. Rich ducked behind and picked up the enchanted, always-full decanter of the tavern's signature spiced coffee.

She poured out a mug. "You look cold still." She waved her hand over the mug and a containment spell formed a spill-proof lid over the steaming liquid, then she pushed it toward Wrenn. "It's on the house."

Wrenn frowned. "You know, if I could figure out how to help with the flashes, I would," she said.

Rich leaned against the counter. "We know." Her eyes narrowed. "You had another flashback, didn't you?" She shook her head. "And Samhain's making it worse, isn't it?"

Wrenn's frown deepened. Sometimes witches knew more than they had a right to.

Rich stood straight and picked up her cloth again. She nodded toward the back room, and presumably Lush. "Lots of us witches have issues, Wrenn. You need to get yours settled or they will eat you up."

Wrenn shrugged and took the coffee. "Yeah." Her witchness would eat her up in a wholly different way than any of the other witches in the realm.

Rich tapped her finger on the smooth wood of the countertop. "*Hmm.*" She went back to wiping the bar, but stopped and stared into the tavern's main room. "You should go home," she said.

Yes, they should both be following the rules. "I have a case." She moved away from the counter so she could tap her paladin star.

Rich continued to stare at the patrons in the main room. "*Hmm,*" she said again.

Wrenn turned around and scanned the fae gathered around the tables and in the game rooms.

There, at a back table, a kelpie shimmered pale green in the low glow along the back wall. He sat alone in the shadows sipping at a pint, with one arm on the back of his chair and his legs out as if he

were looking to trip the waitstaff. He wore a black kilt—they always
wore black kilts—and a tight-fitting black polo shirt. He'd half-heart-
edly swept his black locks back from his face, and one still fell onto
his forehead, giving him a psychotic Clark Kent look.

He wasn't the most beautiful variation of the baseline kelpie look
that she'd seen, but he was handsome enough with the standard kelpie
strong jaw and five o'clock shadow. They all were. Kelpies were pretty
much identically ideal in their features, fantastic to behold and
bewitching, but they were murderous dark fae.

They mostly stayed in Titania's realms, but one or two came into
Oberon's Castle during festivals. They rarely caused overt problems—
dark fae were watched—but that didn't mean this one was behaving
himself. He might just be out on a Samhain jaunt, but Wrenn
suspected not.

She looked back at Rich.

"He's…" Rich blinked. "He's been here all evening," she said.

She blinked again.

Wrenn looked back at the kelpie, then at Rich and her continued
blinking. She shook slightly and went back to wiping at the bar.

Somewhere in the back, a group of fae broke into song. Near the
door, another laughed. The kelpie sat in the shadows sprawled out
like a bored child, watching it all.

Wrenn looked back at Rich, who smiled. "Need a refill?" she asked
as if she'd forgotten that she'd just filled Wrenn's mug.

Which she might have. Wrenn looked back at the kelpie.

The bastard winked.

He'd enthralled Rich to ignore him.

"Want me to get rid of the kelpie?" Wrenn would have to be careful. A kelpie who felt slighted would always look for revenge. They
were as petty as boggarts in that respect.

Rich nodded, blinked again, then went back to her wiping.

Wrenn stood. She smoothed her jacket, made sure her paladin star
was visible, and walked toward the kelpie's corner.

He didn't look at her when she pulled out a chair. He sipped his
pint, watched the satyrs tossing hatchets in the back room, and

ᶠ puffed out his chest. He set down his mug and looked up at her expectantly.

She dropped her hand to her Paladin star without saying a word.

Something was off about this kelpie. He wasn't exuding the charm and charisma that normally acted as their lure.

This kelpie was cold.

"Nae witches out on Samhain." He returned to staring at the game players in the back room and didn't look at her. "Company policy."

Something about her time with Victor kept Wrenn from being read as *witch* by other magicals. Robin speculated it was the same interference that kept them from reading her magical heritage, and also why she didn't overheat the same way the vast majority of witches did, no matter whose magic they semi-wielded.

So to this kelpie, she should have read as mundane. Yet she didn't.

He looked up at her and smiled.

Fangs.

"Out vampire huntin' tonight, darlin'?" he asked.

CHAPTER 4

The proof Wrenn needed of vampires in Oberon's Castle had walked into her neighborhood tavern, gotten himself a pint for show, and sat down waiting for her to come around.

Though he wasn't proof of anything, really, beyond the poor judgment of kelpies. They were as likely to get themselves into dangerous situations as they were a danger for their mundane prey.

Which was the way of dark fae. Stupidly-evil is as stupidly-evil does. And this one was stupid enough to walk around in public.

She shouldn't engage. She should call for backup and have his vamped-out butt hauled into headquarters so he could be properly interrogated by a fae wielding strong magic.

But headquarters might not ask the right questions. Headquarters might dust him the moment backup appeared.

"Tonight's the night you move around the realms undetected, huh?" she asked.

He rubbed the tip of his nose with his thumb knuckle. "Or mayhap I'm just another witch's Samhain vision, sweetheart." He nodded toward the back room.

He'd have to be three witches' vision for that to be true. "If you were a vision, we would have conjured up a handsome kelpie."

His lip twitched and he flashed a fang again.

So he was a hotheaded vamped-out kelpie. She'd have to be careful with the insults.

He silently shifted in his chair—more glided or slipped than shifted—and leaned forward over the table. "Leave me alone an' allow me a moment t' enjoy the ambiance."

"All dark fae are to be surveilled while in Oberon's Castle," she said. Best not to tell him that his fangs meant a dusting once she called him in.

He rolled his eyes. "It's Samhain."

"I could stake you right here and now and be within my rights as a paladin," she said.

He laughed. "Ye think I'm nae real." A wave in the ambient magic moved out from his body. No new magic appeared, only the ripple that hit her and bounced back to him.

So that's how it works, she thought. A true vampire's enthrallings weren't visible in the magic. But this vamp was also a kelpie.

"Get up." She pointed at the exit as she pulled out her phone to call him in. "The Royal Guard would like to know how you got yourself vamped."

He didn't move. "I'm wi'in my rights here." He picked up his pint again. He may have been sipping at it, but it was full still. He hadn't been drinking.

Technically, yes, he was within his rights. Dark fae might be surveilled, but they were common and mostly left alone as long as they didn't indulge their darker behaviors while within Oberon's Castle.

She whipped the chair around and sat with the chairback between them. "I take it you're someone's experiment?" Being someone's experiment counted as a dark behavior.

The kelpie set down his pint.

His fingers drummed on the table in a soundless smooth wave. When she looked back at his face, he'd curled his lip enough to show yet more fang.

Wrenn pulled out her phone. She opened her recording app and aimed the microphone at the kelpie. "You *have* to tell me how you got yourself vamped. I bet it's the best dark fae origin story *ever*."

A low groan rolled from the kelpie.

"Let me guess," Wrenn said. "You tried to enthrall some meek lass but you weren't paying attention and ended up almost sucked dry by one of those vampires who preys on magicals." Wrenn nodded. "But she liked your lovely face and your lovelier abs and now you're some depraved Gulf Coast clan's boy toy." Now she sniffed. "Because none of the *real* European clans would give a shit about a kelpie."

He moved so fast she didn't see him come over the table and grab the back of her chair. "Watch yer mouth," he said.

Wrenn didn't flinch. She stared at the kelpie's lovely ice green eyes. "Do you know why I'm a paladin?" she asked.

He slid back into his chair. "I'm nae from around here."

Kelpies lived in Queen Titania's realms. Seemed she liked all stallions, even the murdering kind.

"Obviously," Wrenn said.

He grinned. No fangs this time, at least.

"I don't thrall." She didn't. "You won't like the taste of my blood, either." Vampires found her "difficult."

Yet another bit of resilience she could hang on Victor Frankenstein.

"Steadfast an' sturdy," he muttered.

"Who do you work for?" She might as well be straightforward.

He chuckled again. "Who said I worked for anyone?"

She shrugged. "Kelpie boy toy, remember? Not one of you is smart or powerful enough to run anything beyond your loch."

"Some o' us are." He breathed out a long string of Gaelic swear words which, if they hadn't come from the mouth of a kelpie, would have been more entertaining than frightening.

Then another wave pulsed out from his body, but not toward her. He pulsed out to the tavern.

He was fast, but so was she. They were both up and with a hand on the other's throat before the enthralling wave reflected back to the kelpie. They were the same height, though he was significantly wider at the shoulders and longer-limbed. He gripped her with ease. She had to twist her shoulder toward him.

"Threatening one of Oberon's paladins is enough to bring you in," she said.

"Goadin' a dark fae is enough t' get ye killed," he answered.

Wrenn reached into her pocket with her free hand, pulled out her phone, thumbed open her camera app, activated the vampire filter, and made a point of taking a picture of the kelpie's head and her hand around his neck.

"That photo willnae show *anythin'*," he growled.

Someone wasn't keeping up with his tech news. She thumbed her Royal Guard app, switched to the front facing lens, and snapped a photo of his hand around her neck.

He grabbed her hair with his other hand.

She stood her ground and snapped another picture.

A full-throated yowl-screech rose out of his throat. No one in the tavern moved. No one noticed. Every single patron ignored them as if they weren't there.

He'd enthralled everyone. She'd underestimated his power level.

And his strength. He pushed her down and to the side. Her knee buckled, and her elbow screamed. She let go of his neck and stumbled to her left, off balance and completely under his control.

She got her phone back into her pocket before he slammed her face into the table. Pain burst outward from her cheekbone and her ear. She pushed on the table to get her footing but he shook her and kept her off balance.

"I ken ye sent in those photos," he slammed her head against the table again to emphasize that he knew exactly what she'd just done. "Do ye think someone's gonnae come to yer rescue? It's almost midnight." He held up her head so she could see the tavern emptying out.

They were all going outside to watch the world move from the light half of the year to the dark.

The kelpie hauled her up again so they were face-to-face. She grabbed his wrist and twisted.

He only laughed. "I came here for th' witch in th' back." He leaned close. "Ye can trade in substantial favors when ye ken what currency is most valuable." He sniffed her ear. "I wonder what one o' yer kind would bring in."

There was only one other of *her kind*. Unless…

"Are you working for him?" One other victim of Victor Frankenstein still walking around. Except the other wasn't a victim. The other was a vampire. "Where is he?"

The kelpie dragged her toward the tavern's back room. "Who, darlin'?" He slapped her hard. "I'm a Gulf Coast boy toy, remember?" He pushed open the door and slammed her against the frame. "Th' rest of the fae, they ken nothin' about what's happenin' in North America." He dragged through another door and into the kitchen. "*Noth—*"

Heat hit her hard. The kitchen had been cleared out but the fires still roared. Meat still sizzled on a spit.

A steel frying pan bounced off the kelpie's face. Iron would have been better, but there was no cold cast iron in the fae realms.

The kelpie swore and let go of her neck and hair.

She grabbed his legs on the way down and toppled him into the kitchen. This time, the wielder of the pan slammed it into the back of his head.

It didn't do any good. The kelpie rolled, kicked her in the face, and swept his arm at the goat-legged fae wielding the pan.

Robin. Oberon's Second-in-Command stood over the kelpie vampire like an adorable sack of horned, sweet boy.

He was in full uniform—midnight blue jacket with silver buttons and a silver hem on the cuffs. Midnight blue trousers tailored to his goat legs. Black shin and hoof guards that acted as boots. A pristine white shirt. Silver caps on his cute horns that set off the room's light as white-hot bolts of glare.

A handsome if stern and self-absorbed face.

A bubble of magic formed around Robin's hands.

There was a reason he'd cleared the staff out of the kitchen. She'd caught the backwash from the last time he'd tossed that spell at a dark fae. She knew exactly what was about to happen.

"Don't!" Wrenn yelled. "He's part of a case I'm working! He knows something about—!"

"No vampires in Oberon's Castle!" Robin interrupted. "You sent in pictures, Wrenn."

"But—"

The ball of magic elongated into a spike. Robin pulled back his arm. And that spike pierced the kelpie's vampire heart.

Light magic blazed. Dark magic roiled. The kelpie-vampire turned into a suffocating dust cloud.

She couldn't see. She couldn't breathe.

"Robin..." she gasped as she blacked out.

CHAPTER 5

Wrenn woke up face down on an ornate parquet floor. Tiny inlays fanned out in a circle in front of her face as if her nose was the epicenter of a wood halo. Intricately-cut bits of oak entwined with equally intensely-meshed teak and mahogany, all of which had been set into the sleek white lines of birch.

And the whole thing smelled of white strawberry varnish.

Which meant she was in one of the large Armory practice rooms. Not her apartment. Not in any of the Royal Guard magic recovery rooms. Not an infirmary or even the kitchen behind Rich and Lush's Tavern.

No. She was in the one place in all of Oberon's Castle where Robin Goodfellow felt comfortable enough to talk about delicate issues.

She rolled over. Long ago, the space had been a ballroom. The parquet flooring and an old stage shimmered in the golden morning sun. A curved balcony ran the entire length of its external wall, separated from the interior by intricately twinkling, intricately cut, leaded-glass doors.

The space was part of the massive towering structure of crystal and obsidian at the center of Oberon's Castle, the actual proper castle of Oberon built a millennium ago. The Armory part was more refurbished rooms like this one, granite blocks, and enchanted fae steel doors rather than the towering grown spires outside.

One needed to be high up in the chain of command to get into the Armory, and Robin Goodfellow was nothing if not a high-hanging link in that chain.

She'd been in this room several times.

Sunshine arced through the space in sheets of rainbow colors from the light thrown by the doors. Reds splashed the walls. Greens danced along the front edge of the stage. Blues and yellows jumped and curved.

All of which camouflaged Robin's natural shimmering magical aura—and his spells.

"What were you thinking, Wrenn?" Robin Goodfellow's deceptively sweet voice echoed off the walls. "On the *holiest* of all the *holy* nights, young lady!"

Wrenn squinted and sat up. The melodrama was a bit much this morning. "Could we not do this, Robin?" she asked. "I need coffee."

Somewhere in the room, he laughed.

Like all the fae in Oberon's Castle, Robin Goodfellow was a sinewy band of flair and subterfuge.

Slowly, she stood. The headache would stabilize in a minute or two, but she'd need either exercise or a few moments in the sun to warm her cold flesh.

A sigil formed just on the edge of her vision, next to her left ear, spinning and pulsing with the power and geometry of the main source of fae power—the natural world. Greens coiled around the sigil's interior designs. Reds nipped at its surface. Cool blues formed its structure.

The sigil was meant to lay a sharp smack across her cheek.

Exercise it would be, then.

She ducked under the slap spell—and twisted away from it, instead of toward where the spell's creator should have been standing.

Something was not right about the spell. The shimmers folded the wrong way, and its tilt felt off, as if she were looking at a reversed photo of a familiar face.

The fae were masters at such deceptions, twisting glamours and flicking out slight-of-hand tricks to deceive a mundane person's senses. Sometimes smells came from the wrong direction, or were off just enough to trigger an unwanted memory. Or a sound echoed in a way that made the mundane think they heard ghosts. Or, with Wrenn, made her see a spell where it wasn't.

The real slap spell grazed her right shoulder. A fiery sting screamed through her leather jacket and into her flesh.

She yipped. The fae used magic to glamour up what they wanted the world to see. She used her reputation. Wrenn Goodfellow, daughter of Puck and Paladin of Oberon. Mundane-born witch, yes, but indestructible. Dangerous. Fast.

Cold. Cutting. Immovable.

The tension from last night's flashback released from its batteries. Her muscles coiled. Bones readied.

Wrenn lowered her shoulder and planted her foot as she scooped her body forward and upward in a one sweeping motion.

Her shoulder hit Robin's belly. She *felt* him, even if she couldn't *see* him or his glamour. Felt her shoulder press into his flesh just under his ribcage. Felt her body take his off-balance weight as she lifted and tossed him away from the sun-kissed balcony doors.

His glamour did not hide the thud when he landed a good six or seven feet away.

What had been heavy air a moment before manifested as Oberon's Second-in-Command lying on the floor like a sack of horned young man.

He still wore his full uniform. Still looked up at her with his handsome if stern and self-absorbed face.

The tension hadn't gone with his flip. It stayed coiled in her leg.

She moved her foot back to kick.

Robin raised his hands. "Good flip!"

Wrenn blinked. The ghosts of her flashback danced just on the edge of her consciousness—there, noticed, yet doing their damnedest to return to hiding behind their own glamour. The tension in her leg moved up into her hips and settled, waiting for a good walk, or a run, or more practice.

She'd almost pummeled Robin's hip, and a kick from her did damage, even to a powerful fae.

"You dusted my lead, Robin." She offered her hand to help him stand.

He nodded and pulled himself to standing. "The boss sniffed a *vampire* in his realms," he said as he smoothed his jacket.

Being a freewheeling Seelie, he would rather prance around naked than in Oberon's new dress requirements.

"Here, of all places!" He shook his head in his melodramatic way. "We'd long suspected they'd try. Turned out turning a dark fae really was the easiest." He snapped his fingers.

"So you were expecting that kelpie?"

Robin looked hurt. "Of course. We figured they'd go after a witch or two first, as well." He waved his hand at the greater air of Oberon's Castle. "I wove detection spells into the witch fire uptake infrastructure a *long* time ago."

Wrenn stared stone-faced at her mentor. "And here I'm the vampire hunter," she said.

Robin rolled his eyes. "Don't be so sarcastic." He fiddled with one of his silver buttons. "I mean, it's all so *obvious*." He waved his hands. "Your photos helped, of course."

No, it wasn't obvious.

In fact, it was so *not* obvious she had a strong suspicion that he was lying. "What other structural obviousness have I been missing, Robin? Since I'm just a witch of unknown origin."

He pouted like a scolded puppy. Then he grinned and pointed at her nose. "You don't overheat when you cast spells." He said it as if he was revealing information she didn't already know. "Strange and sturdy witch that you are."

"And?" she asked.

He leaned toward her as if to tell her a secret. "That means you're difficult to detect while here at home."

Oh, no, she thought. He *had* just shared a secret. He considered her family, but he was still fae, and a powerful one at that.

Now she owed him.

Robin had asked if she wanted a suppression spell for her flashbacks the moment he found her in that dark frozen Scottish forest. He'd sniffed at her person as if he'd detailed every pheromone and fear her body radiated. His eyes had rounded. Then he'd offered multiple gifts of help.

At the time, she hadn't realized who she was dealing with. She only saw a young man, a kid really, who'd been out hunting to help his family. She hadn't wanted to impose on people who were likely living day-to-day. She'd seen too many starving children on the streets of Edinburgh.

Robin had told her later that her selflessness had saved her from his worst tricks.

And with that bit of truth, that tiny bit of revelation, he'd given her a fae boon that tied them together. There was a strange sort of trust between them that had been traded as opposed to earned, but it was there. She literally saw it in his magic every time they were together.

When he'd found her, she also hadn't realized what the shimmer she saw around him meant—or what *she* was.

She knew now, and she used the tactical advantage it gave her every single time she found herself in the presence of a magical—fae, elf, kami, loa, or spirit.

His natural magic pulsed outward, then pulled in closer to his body like armor.

The seeing-magic part of her particular witchdom did have its benefits. "Why do you do that, Robin?" she asked. "The tricks?"

He bunched up his lips and crinkled his nose as if reacting to the imaginary stink of a social slight. "You're so... closed off, Wrenn. These emotions of yours are going to get you killed." He rubbed at his belly before yanking on his jacket hem.

He didn't answer her question.

"Yes, yes. Use my emotions. Don't let them use me," Wrenn said.

They'd had this conversation many times in the past two centuries. "I know."

He tossed her a flicker of side-eye.

She knew what that look meant, as well: The boss had not approved of her adventure last night. Oberon never approved.

So she changed the subject. "I think we have a blood syndicate operating in Oberon's Castle," she said. "Sprites keep washing up, Robin. That kelpie might not be the only vamped-out dark fae walking the realms."

Robin flipped between seemingly hating the constrictions of Oberon's new militaristic dress code and loving the fact that he now had lots and lots of silver bits on his clothes for fiddling and trading.

He stopped playing with his buttons and looked at her. "One kelpie who got himself into a bad situation does not a syndicate make," he said. "You know how dark fae work."

"They're haphazard," she said. "Until someone powerful spins them up into a circuit." Or a syndicate.

Robin's eyebrow arch turned into narrowed eyes and pinched lips.

"I think *he* is part of it."

"That *he?*" He stepped closer and mimed a massive, hulking, fanged demon. "You sure?"

"When are my hunches wrong, Robin?" She rubbed the shoulder she'd used to flip him on his ass.

Robin stared at the light dancing over the doors. "Your hunches are no more statistically significant than anyone else's and you know it."

The modernization of the fae caused interesting science and magic overlaps. The use of statistics, Oberon's Castle public transit, fae wifi and telecommunications—they'd all appeared in the last fifteen years. All of which felt as if Oberon was readying the fae for something.

Robin didn't like it. Once, while drunk, he'd muttered something about privacy and mundanes and a concept called "late stage capitalism." Then he'd downed another jug of mead and thrown up outside the tavern.

He'd still use the tools it offered, though.

He turned toward the sunlit doors and his goat hooves clopped against the wood floor. "Tell me your hunch, Wrenn," he said.

"You know I watch vampiric movements in the mundane world."

He nodded. "Which watching are you talking about?" he asked. "The watching that's part of your job, or the watching you do because you're still obsessed with that demon?"

She narrowed her eyes and pinched the bridge of her nose. "Don't be a jerk, Robin."

He frowned again and bowed his head. "I apologize."

Still, she needed to be careful with him. The last thing she needed was for Robin to snap because he couldn't—or wouldn't—control his own emotions.

But right now, right here in this practice room with its cold lights, with her cold muscles and her achy bones, the last thing she should have to deal with was an immature fae's feelings.

So she stared. No backing down. No words, either. No way for him to twist up what she did in order to fudge his way into extracting another boon or favor, the way he'd done with the secret about the witch-fire uptake system.

Robin's entire body stiffened. "You are angry."

"You asked me to tell you of my hunches. Engaging in an equal sharing of information will help you, Robin." Sometimes she felt more like his mother than his adopted daughter.

He pranced over to the cut glass doors, and with a swoop of his arm, leaned against a particularly dramatic swan.

"Something happened a month ago," he said. "Something that disrupted the vampire status quo." His mouth twisted up. "I've heard rumors of gates opening." His convoluted expression took on a hint of confusion. "Not Heartway gates, so it wasn't us." He glanced off to the side as if thinking about it. "The kami have the power to lure in vampires, but they do not interact with other magicals. At *all.*" He shook his head.

The kami and their various yōkai did, in fact, interact with non-Japanese mundanes and magicals, it just didn't happen often. It wasn't

35

about being insular. Why interact with mundanes who didn't fuel their magic if they didn't have to? Especially vampires.

"So the good money is on elves."

Of course he thought it was elves. With the fae, every bad happening was always the fault of the elves. They were still mad about all those Viking invasions. And the fact that every mundane in the Isles with a sensitivity to magic was descended from that elf princess, and not fae royalty.

But Robin was correct; if it wasn't the fae dealing with their vampire problem, or the kami dealing with theirs, then good money *was* on the elves.

"The fallout seems to be a shift in power," she said.

"*Hmmm...*" he said.

"A shift that has increased the trafficking in magical blood, Robin." Which definitely did *not* indicate elves. Elves did not traffic in anything. They were elves. You got what you saw. When they let you see, which they most often did not.

Everything about Robin's posture said she was correct—the angle of his shoulders, the tension of his neck, the furrowing of his brow.

"I shouldn't..." He trailed off and made a show of slowly rubbing his face as he looked over his shoulder. "You know about the intel dryads."

She nodded. "Samhain was yesterday." Oberon always sent out intelligence gatherers during each of the Eight Festivals. It seemed counter-intuitive, and sacrilegious, but thin veils meant easier spying. And Oberon did like to keep up to date on both enemies and allies.

Robin took her hand. "Come," he said, and pulled her toward the door.

CHAPTER 6

Oberon's actual castle was part granite stonework, part emerged crystal, and part living timber, and it served as one of the anchor points for the layers and layers of interconnected pockets of fae-made lands.

Besides a few stops along the public Heartway transit system, a handful of special locations allowed easy movement out of the fae realms. Most were gateways into the mundane world. Most were mapped. Some were secret and used by royalty. All were used by spies.

The location Robin dragged Wrenn toward sat inside the castle, on a midlevel tier built on top of the intertwined branches of three massive, mighty, east-facing oak trees.

"Why am I here, Robin?" she asked. They'd wound their way through the crystals and onto a boulevard-wide branch of one of the trees.

Robin smoothed his well-tailored uniform. "You are here—" Then he did the same with his luscious black curls, smoothing them away from his cute little horn nubs. "—because the dryads are back."

The intelligence dryads and naiads sent out would trickle back in over the next few days. Two coming in early didn't mean anything.

Robin tossed her one of his prissy looks. He leaned close to her ear. "I sent this pair into elf territory."

"What?" Did the elves really have something to do with their vampire problem? He must have information about the North American enclave who were harboring vampires.

Robin's demeanor subtly shifted from the more personable body language he used with her to his more standard backstabbing prissiness. Robin flicked his wrist and pranced around while wearing his cute glamour as a way to remind the less powerful who was in charge.

He sniffed, but said no more.

Wrenn understood the hint. By sending intelligence dryads into elf territory, Robin might have crossed lines he should not have crossed and any hint might prick problematic ears.

The elves might be fewer in number than the fae, but they were just as powerful. And elves did not freely show their business, nor their magicks.

There were agreements. Nothing particularly binding—the elves were not stupid enough to make deals with the fae—but they did offer each other respect. No nosing around. No spying. General good-neighbor stuff, which it seemed Robin had decided to ignore, and probably rightly so.

Those vampires harbored by the North American enclave might have bitten the elves on the butt. "Did that video of the little elf girl get Oberon to authorize sending in investigators?" Because one part of this puzzle was understanding why elves harbored vampires. Even minor ones.

The elves had wiped the video off the mundane internet almost immediately, but Robin had still managed to get her a copy, mostly because he knew she'd been trying to get any info she could about the enclave.

Robin screwed up his face in an expression that said *maybe, maybe not.*

"What does that mean?" she asked. A video like that, one that sort of revealed the little girl's tall elven ears, could have been a danger to all magicals, not just the elves.

"It means," Robin ushered her into the antechamber of the large, leaf-lined sanctum where the dryads reported, "that the *why* in all this is above both our pay grades."

Very little was above the access that came with the Goodfellow name. "Above our pay grade" did not often apply. She nodded and followed Robin across the shimmering red and green magic gate into the dryads' sanctum.

Robin held his finger to his lips. One did not speak inside the sanctum. One only listened.

Two quick steps and they stood under the massive stones that made up the henge in which the dryads reported. Each stone had been set into the branch's wood, and bark had grown up around their bases, holding them in place.

Two intelligence agents in their antlered armor stood in the center. They mirrored each other's movements, as was their way, and sent their report into the curls of magic flowing through the sanctum like ghosts of an aurora.

The agents told of the elves' land, and a blizzard. Of how, with elves, the forest and its animals lived protected from the pollution and murder of the mundanes, and how the land understood that soon not even its magicals could stop the coming death and damage.

Wrenn shook her head. Mundanes were destructive to the natural world.

The dryads continued: The land spoke of werewolves and elves and witches gone mad. Of concealments they could not read and of wolves masquerading as genies.

Then they spoke of a vampire.

Wrenn shuddered as if she'd fallen under a frozen lake's ice.

It's him, she mouthed to Robin.

Two hundred years out there, probably hiding in caves and feeding on rats, but he'd survived that night in Edinburgh. She now had proof —and evidence that he might still be out there terrorizing the world.

Robin touched his lips again, and leaned his head toward the dryads.

There was another, the dryads reported. A big man who was mundane, yet not. A man who heard the dryads, and saw their magic.

Robin squeezed her hand.

She saw magic. She heard the dryads. And she was mundane, yet not.

This man might have been touched by the same forces Victor had used to make her "viable," as he'd said, and to bring her witch abilities to the surface. He could, like her, be a victim of Victor's experiments.

Or he could be something entirely worse. Something that had survived a supposed death on an Arctic ice floe.

The vampire her captor had created was bad enough, but this man —this *monster*—was why Victor had kidnapped her in the first place. Because he'd wanted a mate.

Wrenn Goodfellow was no monster's bride.

Robin pulled his phone out of his pocket and tapped on the app he used to call up the non-Heartway gateways, the spots only royalty used, then turned it so she could see.

The closest gate to the elves' home was some distance north, situated on a trail inside protected land labeled Paul Bunyan State Forest.

Then he quickly closed the app and stuck the phone back into his pocket.

Thank you, she mouthed. *Send me now. Please.*

Robin frowned.

Residents of Oberon's Castle were supposed to use the Heartway when traveling into the mundane world. Only so many fae could walk the world at the same time, and Oberon was a stickler for this particular rule.

Even his Second had to follow procedure.

Victor Frankenstein had held her captive. He'd unleashed a demigod of a vampire. And he'd lied about the death of his first mistake—a mistake that might have information about his vampiric brother.

Wrenn Goodfellow turned on her heels. She'd never, not once, made others pay for her pain and existence. The men of Frankenstein did.

"Robin…" she whispered.

One of the dryads shrieked.

40

CHAPTER 7

A sparkling orb of light appeared between the dryads.

The dryad on the left tripped as she stepped backward. The one on the right raised her hands to shield her face. A protection spell manifested between the dryads and the orb, but it was too late. The orb exploded outward into a crackling ball of red and green magic.

Someone powerful had interrupted the dryads' report. Someone with enough power they could pop into the sanctum of Oberon's spies without even a tickle from the castle's security spells.

Robin gasped. "What is she doing?"

A feminine hand shot out of the ball of light. Fingers grasped the antlered helmet of the shrieking dryad. And then the dryad's entire suit of armor and the ball of light vanished with an audible pop.

The two dryads vanished. Up a side branch past the henge, a sprite hooted in shock, then also vanished.

"What just happened?" Wrenn said. Someone—a heavily magical *she*, from Robin's response—had literally stolen the armor off a spy's back.

The wisps of natural green and red magic floating around the henge wiggled and brightened as if someone had attached jumper cables to the sanctum's giant tree branch.

Robin breathlessly inhaled. "*Oh, no,*" he said.

All the magic around the henge—where the dryads had been standing, Robin's natural shimmer of turquoise and leaf greens, the normal aurora-like sheets of extra blue in and amongst the clouds—all of it—stiffened as if someone with a lot of power had yanked it taut.

Two centuries with the fae and this was the first time she'd sensed panic among the inhabitants of Oberon's Castle. "Who was that, Robin?" Though her instincts tossed out a likely guess.

Her phone buzzed. So did Robin's.

Every phone buzzed. The *whoop* of a siren wailed from somewhere nearby.

Robin pulled out his phone. "There's a breach."

"In what?" she asked as she pulled out her own phone. "The message says to shelter in place." Nothing about a breach, or whose magic might have caused it, or what any of it meant.

Robin looked around as if to locate an escape route.

Her instincts said she was about to be called to fight. King Oberon was about to need his paladins. "If there's a fight, I need to know what I'm dealing with here, Robin."

Plus she still had the tension coiled in her back and legs.

One of Robin's eyebrows pulled up so high his forehead wrinkled all the way up to his little horn nub. A wry smile followed. "We need arms." He pointed back along the branch, toward the wide arch that led back into the castle and ultimately the stores of the Armory.

He wanted weapons. While inside the castle. "Robin…"

The air popped. A gust followed.

A greenish death-stallion manifested in the center of the henge. Demon red eyes blazed. He reared up and pawed the air with his massive hooves.

The stallion brayed out a sonic shriek so loud Wrenn covered her ears.

Someone had released a kelpie in horse form into Oberon's home.

Robin pulled Wrenn to the side. "What has she done now?"

"Who?" Wrenn asked, though she'd already guessed. Only a royal fae had enough power to cause some type of breach, and only one queen had her own private herd of kelpie stallions.

Titania was up to something.

The kelpie whipped his head around as if he had no idea where he was, or why, or how to get his bearings—until he looked directly at Robin.

The kelpie recognized Oberon's Second in Command. He looked up again at the sanctum and his horse body language changed to that of a fae who recognized his surroundings.

"I don't think he was expecting to end up here," Wrenn said.

"Doesn't matter. No kelpies in the castle." Robin pointed at the stallion. "The order came down last night."

So the King had locked down Oberon's Castle to both vampires *and* kelpies.

Which he wouldn't have done if he didn't care about the blood syndicate. Or the vampires. Or the dark fae involved.

A ghost of a sigil formed in front of the kelpie.

Robin gripped Wrenn's arm as he pointed. "The henge," he said. "It's part of the reporting spells. It…" He inhaled as if he'd just realized he was about to tell her a secret.

Available information about the powers of royal fae was slim to none, as was information about their intelligence-gathering spell-work. Wrenn had no idea how the dryads did their slight-of-hand, or how they communicated with the land, or about their armor, or the henge.

They were spies in the service of King Oberon and she would never be in a position to understand the details of their lives.

But she knew enough to know the ghost sigil between her and the kelpie stallion was *not* fae magic.

"Elves," she breathed.

Elves had engaged the Queen and caused her to let loose kelpies. Elves who likely originated in the territory into which the dryads had been sent to spy and probably had something to do with the root of their vampire blood syndicate issue.

And who were likely harboring Victor's other mistake.

Even if they were not the North American elves, any elven magic manifesting inside his castle was enough to infuriate the King.

Robin grabbed her hand. "We need to leave," he said.

Wrenn yanked away. "You need to send me into there." She pointed at the sigil. "*Now.*" She couldn't open a portal into the elves' territory without entering the Heartway. Robin could. "Tell the King you felt the situation called for a paladin."

He pouted just enough to make her worry about his feelings. Not about his health, or hers, but about a slight on his precious satyr honor. "I *can't*, Wrenn. You know that."

Yes, he could. "Yet you gave me information on the closest gate."

His pout flickered into anger, but that quickly ran and hid under the cover of his returning pout. "So you could make an official case." He yanked on her hand.

The kelpie shrieked. He reared up on his death horse hind legs and slammed his front hooves into the elven sigil.

Power burst off the hit, power so strong, so bright and blue, it felt like Victor's lightning rod.

"This *is* an official case!" She pointed at the kelpie.

The sigil vanished, but the kelpie did not. He tossed his head and looked over his shoulder as if peering at someplace other than the henge.

"Damn it, Robin! Send me now!"

Robin yanked her toward the archway into the castle.

The kelpie looked over his shoulder and brayed out a call. Then he jumped between the standing stones of the henge. A rumbling thump filled the entire space when his hooves hit the wood of the branch.

The sound did not match what her mind expected. It echoed correctly inside the cavernous space holding the henge, but the reverberations felt off—and the timing of the echoes—as if it were coming from a significantly farther distance.

The Queen had opened a portal and Wrenn did the dumbest thing she could do while in the presence of a kelpie in stallion form—she ran toward the henge.

"Wrenn!" Robin yelled. "Don't—"

A second kelpie jumped through the rip. Then another. They looked around in much the same way as the first had when he manifested. Unlike him, they didn't immediately get their bearings.

The first kelpie pawed the floor and snorted at the other two. Then he swung his head toward the arch between the sanctum and the rest of the castle.

They were talking to each other, and the first one through—and the biggest of the three—was giving the other two instructions.

"Robin..." Wrenn pointed. "They're up to something."

Walls of golden power manifested on either side of Wrenn. She looked over her shoulder. Robin waved his hand again and the two walls merged into point about ten feet from where she stood.

He'd spun a magical wedge between her and the stallions. It wouldn't stop them from stampeding, but it should divert them around her body. She wouldn't get trampled.

"Run!" Robin took off toward the archway.

Wrenn looked back at the wedge and the kelpies streaming by. They growled and wailed, and split around the magic *moving* walls.

The wedge followed Robin like a puppy, forcing her away from the kelpies' portal.

"Damn it." Wrenn ran after Robin.

The two smaller pale green bodies pressed against the wedge on either side as she ran, with the biggest one pushing from behind. Red demon eyes glared down. White sparks snapped every time magic touched magic. And each hoof strike on the branch caused another reverberation, another echo, that merged with their white sparks and red eyes.

Wrenn couldn't breathe. She couldn't see, or think, or move well enough to get away.

The two smaller kelpies galloped through the archway between the reporting henge and the rest of the castle.

Robin's magical wedge, though, had other plans. It must have interacted with a containment spell set to hold in the kelpies because she ran face first into a doughy wall of magic.

The largest kelpie also slammed against the wedge-shield and the air oscillated. She fell backward, out of Robin's magic shield and directly under the keystone of the arch, but still on the henge side. The grand stone rose up to her left, curved over her head, and dropped down again on her right.

The barrier shimmered in the golden light streaming in from the henge side and looked more like a thin, stretched-out cloud of pixie dust than anything capable of holding off kelpies.

Which it *hadn't*. The hooves of the second two kelpies clacked against castle stones just outside the archway.

The kelpie with her snorted out an order. The other two looked at each other and galloped down the corridor.

None of Robin's natural magic filled the corridor on the other side of the barrier, so either the kelpies pushed him ahead, or he'd whipped up a strong concealment enchantment. But strong spells took concentration, and time, neither of which had been available.

So it was just her and the particularly menacing kelpie pawing at the floor next to her legs.

He was the size of a draft horse and the same pale sickly green as all the other kelpies. He smelled fresher than most, more like sunshine on a loch than rotting lake weeds. His eyes shimmered with their normal ruby brilliance and he wore a shimmering bridle of champagne gold.

He was quite handsome for a murder pony, charming in a grand Scottish way, and able to kill a lass thirty times over before she drew a breath.

At least this one wasn't a vampire.

He sniffed at her face as if he meant to lick her. Wrenn slapped his muzzle with a protection spell.

He sneezed and wet kelpie breath bounced off her cheek.

Ugh, she thought. Her innate protection magic wasn't strong enough to hold him off for long, but it would keep him from biting. "What's your name, kelpie?" she cooed. All that need to murder tended to make them single-minded and boorish, and sometimes a good fawning pampering put them into a stupor long enough for a lass to get away.

The kelpie pawed at the wood. He pushed his snout into the barrier, then backed off as if it stung.

He used his head to nudge her against the magic.

A heat prickled as her back pressed into what felt like twinkling fairy dust dough with some give, but not a lot. It ballooned out around her sides as if it were about to swallow her whole.

She pulled herself back into the henge side.

The kelpie's ruby red eyes narrowed. He clearly understood what had just happened.

So he was more intelligent than the average kelpie. Big, extra strong, and smart—this one might be royal.

Wonderful, Wrenn thought. "You should probably turn around and go back through that portal before King Oberon takes a personal interest in your marauding," she said.

The kelpie brayed out a laugh.

He was also unsurprisingly arrogant. So arrogant, it seemed, that he felt confident enough to nudge her even though she'd slapped him with a protection spell—and to put his bridle within reach as a result.

If she could steal his bridle, he'd have to do as she asked. Which she might be able to manipulate him into doing anyway. "You were battling elves, were you not?" she asked. "Nothing worse than an elf, huh?"

He sniffed at her face again.

"Is that portal still open?" She pointed around his massive neck.

The kelpie's head came down and he slammed his forehead into her breastbone—and slammed her into the sparkle dough barrier.

Wrenn coughed. She inhaled deeply and allowed her silver and green protection spells to knit around her body. The kelpie wanted to use her as a shield to force his way through into the castle. Maybe she could move her arms well enough to grab onto his bridle? The leather across his muzzle pressed against her front and if she—

The kelpie rammed his head into her chest again. All her breath puffed out into the barrier. Sharp pain radiated up into her neck and down both her arms and out into her protection spells. She instinctively tried to inhale—and got a lungful of burning magic dough.

New hot pain radiated outward from her chest. She was drowning inside barrier magic. The damned kelpie had found a way to drown her on dry land, high up inside a castle, because that's what kelpies did. They dragged you under.

If she was going to asphyxiate on magic, so was the kelpie. No kelpie would get the best of her, no matter how big and strong.

She grabbed the silver rings on either side of his mouth and yanked downward. The barrier magic resisted, puffing up around his muzzle, but enough worked into his nostrils that he tried to snort it out. He tried to buck, but the dough-like mounding of the magic constrained him as much as it did her.

Even in the tight cushioned space, he managed to slam against her again.

Wrenn fell through the barrier magic. Fresh air rushed into her nose and lungs. Burning pain still set every nerve in her body on fire, but she breathed.

And she still had ahold of his bridle. She reached for the strap between his eyes, hoping to yank off the entire assembly.

The kelpie pushed through his head and spit directly into her eyes.

Wrenn yelped. "You just can't help yourself, can you?" She pulled on the bridle's strap.

The kelpie charged through and swung his head at the same time, slamming her against the cold stone of the castle wall.

Her left elbow joint popped.

New white-hot agony manifested in and around the entire left side of her body. Her fingers disengaged from the bridle, not because she let go, but because her left hand stopped working, and her right hand responded with a spasm.

She slid down the cold stone wall to the floor.

The kelpie towered over her, his head up as he sniffed the air, and his bridle still on his head. His front hooves were close enough that he could rear up and trample her where she sat. He could, if he wanted, completely rip off her damaged arm.

He whinnied, then cocked his head as he listened.

Down the hall, another kelpie whinnied a reply.

The kelpie galloped away, toward his comrade, leaving her alone to pop her elbow back into place.

She yelled as she pushed herself off the wall and realigned her joint. Her witch-body resilience would have the pain settling momentarily.

Most of the weapons cache was in the Armory under lock and key. But some of it was not. Some of it was just too magical and too important to the King to have it out where mere acolytes could lay their hands on it.

Some of it needed to be kept close to the royalty.

Wrenn bolted down the corridor after the kelpie and toward the one room in the entire interconnected metropolis of Oberon's Castle that a dark fae should not, and hopefully could not, enter: The Gallery of Artifacts.

CHAPTER 8

R obin had snuck Wrenn into the Gallery of Artifacts once. He'd waved his hand and touched her forehead. Then he'd nodded and said, "There," as if that one word was enough to allow her to transit in and out of all the tiny, hidden pockets within Oberon's Castle.

He hadn't given her that kind of key, of course. After five minutes deep inside the Gallery, his spell had worn off and the room had flung her all the way to the Armory's yard. She'd landed in the middle of a cloud of pixies running tactical drills.

She'd only gotten a glimpse of what was in there—a troll mace the size of her head. An ethereal silver bow, quiver, and arrows. Keys. Several daggers. Fae-made chainmail. Indigo and red kami-made leather and silk armor. Modern-looking leather-and-silver elven body armor that appeared to be more grown than built.

And swords. Hundreds of swords in all shapes and sizes stored on the walls that ran away from the door into what looked like infinity. Swords three kelpies could use to cause all sorts of suffering.

This level of the castle was mostly vast outer rooms surrounding a central column of stairs and elevators. The whole set was high enough up the spire that the curve of the outer hall kept you from seeing more than twenty feet ahead, but you could hear.

Wrenn ran along the inside wall, watching and listening for neighs and brays. Up ahead, clops turned to footfalls and horse noises turned to yells.

The kelpies were shifting to human form.

There was some sort of magical geometry and physics going on in the castle that probably had to do with proximity of pockets of fae-generated realities, the reporting henge, nearness to Oberon's main rooms, and portal access. She'd never been able to consciously discern a pattern, though she sensed one.

So did the kelpies. She rounded the curve to find three handsome dark-haired men in kilts standing in front of a blank space on the inner wall.

Except it wasn't blank, and they weren't alone.

The biggest of the kelpies in human form—he was a good four inches taller than Wrenn, and looked to be carrying at least half-again her body weight in pure muscle—held Robin by the scruff of his neck.

They'd tied his hands with a black leather belt to keep him from zapping out spells, and from the looks of it, had smacked him against the wall enough times to stun him into semi-consciousness.

All three kelpies wore the same black polo shirt with the same little silver-green horse embroidered over their left pec. All wore matte black tactical kilts covered with pockets and body armor panels. Even their boots were black, though their socks were the same pale green as the little horse emblems.

They were also almost physically identical, except for a fair size variation. All had handsome square jaws, the same glorious ebony curls hanging over their foreheads as had the vamped-out one in the tavern, and enough of a five o'clock shadow to accentuate high levels of testosterone.

All had twisted leather straps tied around their necks. Each strap threaded around multiple silver rings.

Their bridles.

They were all things kelpie—dumb, pretty, arrogant, and dangerous.

"You know who that is, don't you?" Wrenn pointed at Robin.

The huge kelpie scowled like a toddler. "That th' lass, Ranger?" he asked the much smaller one standing to his left.

The smallest of the three, the one the big one called Ranger, sniffed the air. "She tried t' steal my bridle, lads."

So the massive draft-horse-sized kelpie turned into a squat little human.

A chorus of *ohhhhs* and *ahhhs* rose from the group.

Ranger pointed at Wrenn. "Run awa' now, ye ugly sow, before we thrall ye an' smash yer brains like we're doin' t' the goat boy."

The big one held up Robin and gave him a shake.

"The King's going to have your heads," Wrenn said.

The three kelpies laughed. "We're th' Queen's stallions." They all puffed up their chests as if they truly thought being the Queen's favorites would save them from Oberon's wrath.

She pointed at Robin. "That's *Puck*, you morons," she said.

The big one peered at Robin's face. "All th' goat boys look th' same."

Ranger shrugged. "Th' fat ugly one thinks we care."

How many times in her life had she heard that exact insult? You're too tall. You're too strong. No one wants a woman your size.

"The Shire horse thing was compensation, huh?" Wrenn held up her thumb and forefinger about an inch apart.

Red demon fire shot horizontally out the sides of Ranger's eyes. "We lucked intae this, boys!" He tapped the wall. "I scent th' power."

Robin stirred. "You are not allowed—"

The big one rammed his head into the wall.

"Stop!" Wrenn yelled. They might actually hurt Robin with all the slamming.

The one called Ranger ignored her pleas and ran his hand over the wall.

The concealment spell hiding the Gallery of Artifacts cracked like glass. A splinter fell off and clinked to the floor as if it had been made from the finest leaded crystal like the doors to the practice room.

A ball of magic formed around Ranger's fist and he, too, hit the wall.

The entire spell shattered.

Wrenn cringed. A claxon alarm bonged.

Ranger dashed through the opening. The big kelpie dropped Robin and followed. The other one looked at Wrenn, then at Robin.

"What are you idiots trying to steal?" Had that vamped kelpie said anything about kelpie artifacts? She couldn't remember. "Who are you working for?"

The remaining one made a rude gesture, then also sprinted into the Gallery of Artifacts.

Wrenn ran to Robin. "You okay?" She untied his hands as she watched the kelpie disappear around a stand of staves.

She looked around. "Where's the Royal Guard?" Someone with authority to enter a walled-off pocket of terrible weapons should have shown up by now.

Robin pulled himself to his hooves. He slapped a hand against her forehead then pushed her toward the hole in the wall and the new entrance in the Gallery. "I'll tell the King the situation required a paladin."

Without a fae guide, she could get stuck in there. "But..."

A ball of magic formed around his hand and he tossed her through.

CHAPTER 9

The fae were particularly good at spellwork that warped space and time. It was pretty much all they did—or at least all they pretended to do. Casting an illusion of doing the warping and bending was usually as good as actually doing the work.

Illusions saved magical energy. Saved energy provided a strong tactical advantage—an advantage often nullified by her ability to see magic.

Nine times out of ten, Wrenn Goodfellow could tell illusion from structural spellwork. Inside the Gallery of Artifacts, the illusions *were* the structure.

The inside of the Gallery was at least ten times bigger than the room's possible space, and extended so far from the entrance that the back wall was not visible. It wasn't, though. Wrenn knew it wasn't, yet it was.

The only explanation that made any sense was that the Gallery was a small pocket realm anchored to the castle. As a realm, its internal space didn't fit into the room where it "lived." And just to make things more fun, the realm itself was full of illusions making it look and feel significantly bigger than it actually was.

And all the illusions served as alarms, tricks, and traps.

She looked over her shoulder at Robin on the other side of the hole. He must have done something to hide her from the guard spells inside the Gallery. She looked back at the three kelpies disappearing between the display cases.

They, too, hadn't set off the alarms.

To her left, a row of modern-looking display cases formed a line into the endless shadows at the far end of the Gallery. Behind the cases was a wall full of mostly bows and arrows, with a gun or two thrown in.

These were not the displays around the entrance. When Robin had brought her in before, the antechamber had a wide arch over an open display floor. Everything there had been fae in origin, and of the exquisite work Oberon liked to show off.

Every single object in this area glowed with magical light, some so brightly she had a difficult time telling if the object was a blade, or an arrow, or even a whip. Most of the objects carried multiple layers of magic beyond their inherent enchantments.

More of the alarms and traps. Some were glowing so brightly because they were purposefully hidden under an illusion, like the mask in the display case just inside the door. It looked kami, but she could tell immediately that it wasn't—someone had tooled leather to look like a blue demonic oni, but it wasn't a real oni, nor was it even a good fake. And the magic around it was one hundred percent fae.

But it grabbed her attention. She tried to look around, to perhaps spot the real kami artifact it was meant to help conceal, but the bright blue color and the flat-out gall of such fakery made her want to punch the display case.

Which was probably the point.

She turned her back to the mask.

And there, directly across from the overtly melodramatic display of a fake kami artifact, was another display case, this one holding an obviously fake dolphin-headed Viking arm ring. It, too, made her want to hit the case.

So in this part of the Gallery, guard spells went full-in on the contempt of all the other magicals. Every single display case here was full of distractingly audacious bits of illusion meant to piss off pretty much anyone who got this far inside.

The kelpies had run right by.

In the shadows at the far end of the Gallery, a kelpie kicked another case.

"Hey!" she yelled as she shaded her eyes from the magical glare permeating the Gallery. How much power would this merry band of morons gather to themselves if they stole heavily enchanted weapons? She looked over her shoulder again. When would the castle Royal Guard—

She turned her head back to look into the Gallery and the big kelpie hit her with a straight-on jab to her nose.

Something cracked and pain blossomed from the bridge of her nose, but she didn't falter. She slid her foot back and held her ground.

Wrenn wiped away a drip of blood and sneered at the kelpie over the back of her hand.

He blinked, and for a second he looked frightened.

Her nose had already begun to reset itself. "We're not near your loch, you dumbass," she said. "So what little enthralling ability you might have had over me, you most certainly do not have here."

For a fraction of a second the huge handsome kelpie, the one who was clearly stronger than the other two, jutted out his lip like a toddler. Then the rage hit. Red demon fire blazed from the sides of his eyes. He grabbed her jacket and swung her into the display case with the fake elven arm ring.

The hit felt as if she'd bounced off concrete. The case didn't crack.

It moved, though.

"Ranger!" The kelpie yelled. He picked her up to swing her against the case again.

Wrenn lifted both her feet off the ground. She tightened her back. And all that pent-up energy from her flashback released as a two-footed kick. One heel hit his lower abdomen. The other, his crotch.

His breath billowed out of his mouth as a high-pitched wail. He dropped her against the shifted case.

Wrenn rolled into the shadows between the case and the wall of blades behind it.

The kelpie bellowed. One of his mates, somewhere deep in the Gallery, responded with a chorus of brays.

At least one had changed back into his stallion form. If this one changed, his next stomp would do real damage.

She needed a weapon.

Every blade in the Gallery glowed with fae magical fire so bright she had a difficult time discerning where the blades ended and the grips and pommels began, but under all those fae concealment and illusion spells she picked out the truth: All the blades on this section of wall had been forged by the elves from elven silver and steel. All carried Norse runes and elven enchantments. And every single sword and dagger looked strong enough to cut a kelpie in half.

One sword glowed less than the others and she could make out its true size and shape. It was the biggest Viking sword she'd ever seen, bigger than most claymores, and with tightly woven emerald-green magic over its leather-covered grip. And it looked sharp enough to split a tree in two.

Wrenn jumped to a crouch and grabbed the sword's hilt.

The emerald magic puffed out in much the same dough-like way the barricade enchantment between the henge and the castle had, but instead of forcing her to drop the sword, it glommed onto her hand as if the sword had tied itself to her with silk.

"*Heh,*" she said. "I think you like me." Maybe she really was a witch of elven descent.

The big kelpie bellowed, and in a blink of an eye, went from big man to thoroughbred-sized horse.

Wrenn held the sword between her and the stallion. "What do the Scandinavians call your kind? *Bäckahäst,* correct?" She twirled the sword. "Elves do *not* like dark fae."

Deep in the Gallery, another kelpie whinnied. Mr. Big raised his head and whinnied back. Then he snorted at Wrenn and ran toward his companions.

One of them found what they were looking for, she thought, and bolted after the kelpie stallions—until Ranger, still in human form, barreled into her from the side.

They both flew into a rack of staves. Rods and poles, most with metal caps, clanked and clattered to the floor. Ranger stomped his foot down onto her wrist holding the sword, trying to force her to let go, and grabbed her by the hair.

Thank goodness she didn't get a view up his kilt. She did, though, get whopped in the jaw by one of the kilt's armored plates.

"Get off me!" she roared. Damned disgusting kelpies. Why did the Queen keep an entire stable full of them? They were as shallow and evil as vampires.

A blast of magic hit Ranger's head. He yipped and fell to the side, panting and mumbling as if the spell had scrambled his mind.

Wrenn kicked him in the gut and rolled to a crouch.

Robin stood a few paces away, framed in the glow of the gap in the wall and leaning against one of the undamaged display cases. "Put that back." He didn't move, or point, or indicate in any way that he meant the sword.

She held it up. "This?"

He looked up just as one of the kelpies galloped right into him and the display.

The case smashed to the floor. Robin somehow danced out of the way. And behind them, the third kelpie dashed through the gap and back into the castle.

He ran headfirst into a new concealment enchantment meant to close off the Gallery from the rest of the castle. And standing out there in the hallway, at least five members of Oberon's personal Royal Guard held up their hands to cast a new enchantment at the Gallery of Artifacts.

"They're going to vent the Gallery," Robin said.

"What?" They weren't in a spaceship. Though in some ways they were, because of how the spells manipulated space, but this place was magic, not science.

Robin moved his hands. A spell formed. "You need to go," he said.

"What about you?" she asked.

He looked back at the Royal Guard. "I'll be fine."

He wouldn't. "You're hurt."

Robin's eyes flashed from the handsome blue of his glamour to a starscape of black. The horn nubs on his head brightened, and suddenly he carried a full set of massive curved goat horns. He grew in height. His goat legs elongated and grew thicker, darker fur.

His uniform changed from the midnight blue militaristic jacket and boot-like foot coverings to something black and coiling as if he wore a coat of living night.

A portal opened to her side.

When she looked back, he'd reverted to his young glamour. "Go!" he said.

"Rob—"

Ranger tackled her into the portal.

CHAPTER 10

Alfheim County, Minnesota, the mundane world...

Eduardo Martinez leaned against his cruiser and watched the golds, pinks, and purples of the post-blizzard sunset spread over the remaining clouds. The sun had burst out from behind the gray clouds early mid-morning and had started the normal freeze-thaw cycle that always happened after a big storm this time of year. What had been snow on the roads turned to mush, which was now turning into a slick layer of ice.

He'd already handled more accidents today than he usually did the entire summer. The one about to be hauled away by Gullinbursti Reclamations' tow truck would hopefully be his last for the day.

Bill waved from the cab of the truck. Ed waved back, and then to the two tourists who'd spun their Audi into the ditch on the other side of the road. They were an older couple whose youngest had just started college, and they'd come up north for Alfheim's Halloween festivities.

The festivities around here were more Samhain than Halloween, but "the mundanes" didn't need to know that, as the elves like to say.

Ed rubbed at his stocking cap's Alfheim County Sheriff's Department logo, situated on his forehead like some sort of authoritative third eye—which wasn't as authoritative with the locals as he liked.

He'd been on duty for almost a full twenty-four hours. He'd caught a few naps in his cruiser, but between the fright with his daughter last night, the blizzard, the werewolves and their run, the elves and Samhain, all the traffic problems...

The tourist wife had said it was a brand-new Audi and they hadn't quite gotten the feel of it yet. Then the husband shrugged and launched into a story about the good old days and the Great Halloween Blizzard of '91.

Bill would take the car into Magnus Freyrsson's dealership, and the shuttle would take them to the resort where they were staying, which also happened to be owned by Magnus Freyrsson. They'd get a complimentary bottle from the local winery and a calming massage from one of the elves who worked in the resort's spa.

And then this wealthy couple who spent most of their days crunching numbers for one of the big banks in St. Paul would be so charmed they would never again spend tourism dollars somewhere not elf-approved.

And thus was the way of Alfheim, and in particular, the way of the local elven aspect of the Norse god Freyr.

Ed waved again as Bill, his truck, and the drive-train-addled Audi pulled away.

There'd be more ice on the roads overnight. Probably another accident or two. He rubbed at his head again. Minnesotans like to talk up how good they were on ice—and they were, mostly—but come the first real storm of the season and half the state ended up with busted taillights, smashed bumpers, and whiplash.

Ed squeezed his hands and shook out his fingers. His gloves did their job—they'd been charmed by the local Elf Queen herself—and he would never suffer frostbite or even a chilly tingle. The elves always charmed his family's winter gear. Said it was one of the perks of being one of the handful of mundanes in town who understood magic. But mostly it seemed a bit paternalistic.

Still, none of his kids ever got cold toes.

They were all home today, with school called, after last night's ordeal.

He dialed home.

Gabriel, his soon-to-be thirteen-year-old, answered. "Papa!" he said.

"Just pulled the last tourist out of a ditch," Ed said.

Rustling echoed through the connection as Gabe grabbed his tablet. "Ready," he said.

"Audi A8L," Ed said.

"*Ohhhhh….*" Gabe responded. "Not bad."

Ed chuckled. Gabe had a friend in Grand Marais he'd met in 4-H and they were collecting data about tourist spending in Alfheim versus what they spent up on the North Shore.

Ed didn't know how "cars driven by tourists who get into accidents" fit into the whole giant science-fair-board of a presentation, but Gabe seemed to be enjoying collecting the data. "Brand-new, too. Less than five hundred miles on it."

"That's a shame," Gabe said. "Mr. Freyrsson's people will fix it right up." He paused. "Brandon says Cook County had only three accidents."

Brandon was his friend in Grand Marais who was funneling Gabe North Shore stats.

"Do you think the… locals… have something to do with the higher accident rate here during storms?" Gabe asked.

They did not use terms like "magical" or "elf" or "werewolf" when communicating in any way other than face-to-face. Even a hint getting out about anything out of the ordinary would cause repercussions.

What those repercussions might be, Ed didn't know, mostly because no one had ever leaked the existence of elves to the wider world.

It was all very circular, the control the elves had on Alfheim County.

"*Hmm…*" Ed said.

"They might not realize," Gabe said. "It might not be intended."

Excitement peppered his voice. "Wouldn't it be cool if I found something they didn't know about?" He shuffled something around. "I'm going to put together a presentation for Mayor Tyrsdottir."

No asking permission. No running it by the elf at school who ran the 4-H program. Just an "I'm gonna point this out to the Elf Queen of Alfheim," as if they would hold young Gabriel Martinez in high enough esteem to listen.

Dagrun Tyrsdottir would listen. Then she'd tell Ed to get real stats, and that would be the end of it because they probably did know, and the knowing part was way above Ed's pay grade, much less his son's.

Gabe presenting the data in a coherent form, even if it never led to a decrease in traffic accidents in Alfheim County, would at least look good for future college applications. "Call her office once it's ready," Ed said.

"I will," Gabe said. "Can I get official accident reports? Legally, I mean?"

Ed rubbed at the logo on his hat again. "Let's talk about that later." They had a lot to talk about, his family. About last night. About what was happening with Gabe's sister, Sophia. About the new baby and the very real chance that Ed might be dealing with the tourists from The Cities on their home turf sometime soon.

But he and Isabella hadn't talked to the kids yet about the possibility of leaving Alfheim for the Greater Minneapolis-St. Paul Metropolitan Statistical Area.

"Okay," Gabe said. "Are you going to be home for dinner? Jax and his mom brought over *digaag duban*, rice, and cardamom cookies so Mom wouldn't have to cook."

"Axlam's up?" Ed asked. That woman should still be sleeping off last night's run. But then again, there was a reason Axlam Geroux was an alpha werewolf.

"They stopped by to make sure Sophia was okay."

Of course they did. He wouldn't hear a damned thing about the whole episode from the elves until Samhain was fully in their rearview mirror, but the wolves? Axlam was *injured*, for goodness sake, and yet she and her boy showed up to check on his family.

Though after seeing Frank Victorsson and his mysterious girl-friend at Magnus Freyrsson's place, Ed suspected the elves had one of their elf things going on.

Ed knew enough about Norse mythology to have a not-so-good feeling about the number and level of "elf things" happening lately.

Yet another good reason to pack up his family and move down to the suburbs.

Or maybe back to Texas. Houston had good schools, apart from the Texas need to edit history to their white advantage. The University of Minnesota was a damned fine school though, and resident tuition was a lot cheaper, and they only had five years before that whole expense clicked on. And the elves had promised to help pay for all five of his kids.

He'd also have to talk to the elves about that number, too.

He rubbed the hamburger-like scar on his neck. He needed to remember that this place was safer for him and safer for his family than any place in Texas, Houston included.

Ed looked out over the trees and snow. Ten years in Alfheim County, Minnesota, nine-and-a-half of those as Sheriff, and he still found the elves as annoying as he found the tourists.

His radio clicked. "Sheriff Martinez?" Tracy at dispatch said.

"Got a call," Ed said to Gabe.

"All right, Papa. Bye." His son hung up.

Ed pressed the button on his mic and leaned his head toward his shoulder. "Go ahead," he said.

"So," she said in her thick Northern Minnesota accent no one here admitted to having, "looks like the State Patrol's needing backup up in the Paul Bunyan State Forest. They're tied up with that last accident on 34 and are about half-an-hour out."

Ed settled into his cruiser. Why were they calling him? Alfheim County only contained the southern tip of the park. "No one from Hubbard available?" Hubbard County contained the rest of the territory.

"Well, yes, but..." She paused. "State Patrol's responding but you're closer and it's a guy in a... kilt... and a woman dressed all in black, sir."

Tracy's husband was a werewolf, so she was keyed into the local magic.

Kilt? The pauses meant she suspected they were dealing with a Scottish magical. Most likely a fae, and probably not a nice one, either.

"The woman's got a sword." Tracy paused again. "It's, ah, *large*, sir."

And here he thought he would be able to go home and have himself a nice meal of tasty homemade Somali baked chicken.

Guess not, he thought.

"I'm on my way," he said as he turned his cruiser north toward the Paul Bunyan State Forest.

CHAPTER 11

Paul Bunyan State Forest...

Movement across the veil into the mundane world hurt. The Heartway, because it was scaled-up and homogenized and she was a witch, demanded a token.

Sometimes the Heartway demanded more than the value of the token she paid for in coin. Sometimes it demanded user fees rendered in distilled pain.

Some fees came as a sharp stabbing pain in her lower back. Sometimes the process wanted actual blood. Once, when she hadn't had enough for a full fare, the Heartway had ripped open her flashbacks as payment. She'd ended up sitting on the steps of a small church outside Dublin weeping quietly under a midnight Irish moon.

All because she was not fae. All because witchdom was an affront to the natural order of things and all those who carried magic in a resisting mundane body had to spark and overheat and lose their minds.

Because if you sparked, you had to pay in extra pain.

But this time her movement wasn't via the Heartway. This time Robin had flung her through a portal of his own making.

So her one and only token would not be accepted. All pain must be handed over on demand.

And all her pain came back to Victor Frankenstein in one way or another.

The moments inside a veil between realms were as endless as they were instant. Entire lifetimes happened in a crossing, birthing into the veil, running their course to your last breath as you pushed on through to the other side. Lives felt as cold shivers up a spine in the middle of the night, or the ghostly touches felt when breathing spring air, or the savory roasting of fall meats.

They happened, yet they didn't, and every single one of Wrenn's crossings grazed the life of Victor Frankenstein.

There'd been goodness there, once. A love for a mother who doted and who served as the needed scaffolding to hold together Victor's distracted and consumed mind. A scaffolding he genuinely required because his was not a mind that held itself holistically to any project, no matter how he waxed poetic about the sublime, or nature, or his supposedly deep understanding of life and death. Victor would find himself consumed with a task, focused only on it, to the detriment of his health and the health of all those around him. And when his mother died, that compassionate structure crumbled, so he turned to the only other structure available to him at that time: his titles and wealth.

A great person once said that with great power came great responsibility, and Victor Frankenstein was not a man who did well with any responsibility, great or small.

By the time he'd kidnapped Wrenn—and she was sure he'd kidnapped her, no matter how he claimed he'd been saving her from worse circumstances—he'd sunk so low into his own misery that he thought it perfectly acceptable to destroy her memories of her previous life. He'd resuscitated her, he'd said, because there was a fiend out there who demanded nothing less than a perfect bride. A terrifying fiend, one so horrid and horrible that Victor couldn't—no, *wouldn't*—allow him anywhere near Wrenn.

But it was her job to remember that she'd drowned. He'd brought her back from the edge of death, and she should be grateful.

He'd left evidence about the fiend—detailed journals of the monster's stalkings. About little William's death, and Justine, and his friend Henry. About the Orkney Islands and the death of a wife named Elizabeth.

So there were truths inside Victor's misery. But they weren't the most important truth for Wrenn.

Victor had resuscitated her because he thought he could mold a woman without memories into a figure who doted on him and would serve as his missing scaffolding. A woman who loved him. A woman all his own.

The Victor she'd known had fallen down a well of sin and had decided that splashing around in the dark, cold wetness of his soul was all that was left to him, no matter what ropes were thrown to pull him out.

He only wanted to pull her in with him.

And then he built a demon.

Wrenn Goodfellow gasped awake as she dropped out of the veil between Oberon's realms and into the frigid winter air of the mundane world. All air.

Just air.

She was a good one hundred feet above the ground and dropping fast into a vast stand of fifty- to sixty-foot trees.

The portal had opened *over* a forest. High up over a forest.

Enough light spread from the setting sun to throw dark shadows, making the forest look thicker than it was and making it difficult to tell if the cedar directly below her was strong enough to usefully break her fall. If she grabbed a limb, or swung the sword...

The emerald magic wrapped around the hilt and her hand pulsed once, and she was sure the sword woke up.

Her legs hit the top of a cedar. She flipped over, now dropping headfirst, and rolled toward the trunk.

Her back hit a bigger branch. A loud crack shook the tree, though thankfully not her bones, even if it did knock her breath from her body. She flipped over again and swung the sword at the next branch.

The blade cut clean through the wood.

The branch snapped downward faster than she fell, slamming against the tree before bouncing down to the ground.

She fell again, but this time she jabbed the sword into the trunk. It sliced all the way through, the tip of the blade visible on the other side, and cut downward for a good five feet before it, and Wrenn, stopped descending.

She was still about seven feet up and hanging from the hilt of a magical Norse sword.

"Thank you," she whispered to the blade she somehow knew was also a *she*.

A she named Red.

"What?" Wrenn muttered. "Are you talking to me?" she asked the blade.

No answer. Nothing at all, as if Red had decided to go back to being a simple magical sword. Which she clearly wasn't. Not with the layer upon layer of magic wrapping her hilt and blade.

What did I steal from the Gallery? Wrenn thought.

No answer.

The golden glow of a northern sunset sparkled off icy rocks and snow. The temperature was most definitely below freezing. And the trees looked North American.

Had Robin tossed her into the Paul Bunyan State Forest near the North American elven enclave? What about Ranger?

Where was that damned kelpie?

Two trees over, hanging over the stout branch of a pine with his well-shaped butt fully exposed to the wind, was the unconscious Ranger.

"Kilts aren't built for dropping into the north country, now are they?" she snickered.

Now to get herself down before he woke up.

She wrapped her legs around the closest branch. It wasn't all that sturdy, but if she stayed next to the trunk, she could use it for stabilization until she figured out how to maneuver down to the ground.

The branch creaked but held. Wrenn left Red where she was for the moment, and pulled out her phone.

She held it up.

The phone's enchanted circuitry folded in on itself as she watched. All her fae-fueled apps vanished from her screens and were now sequestered inside a passcode-protected "game" app. To a mundane person, her phone would look like everyone else's, and it would take a true magical to sense that it was fae-built.

She held the phone up higher.

And there, a very weak signal from a mundane carrier.

She tapped at the real-world mapping app.

Robin had in fact dropped her into the Paul Bunyan State Forest, but from the looks of it, she was a good three kilometers from a place called Manny's Backwoods Lodge, the building that housed the actual spy-used local access gate.

She tucked away her phone. She'd have to drag a cold-assed kelpie three kilometers to take him back to Oberon's Castle.

A roaring buzz bounced through the trees. Three beams of light followed.

Snowmobiles coming in from the east.

Ranger stirred.

Wrenn yanked Red out of the tree. "All right, hon, let's do this," she said, and leaned down far enough so she could jab the sword back into the trunk no more than five feet off the ground.

She swung down, one hand on the hilt and the other on the pommel, until she dropped her boots onto the cold ground.

Wrenn pulled Red out and trudged her way through the crispy snow toward Ranger's tree.

He looked up and shaded his eyes as he peered at the approaching snowmobiles. "No lasses," he said. "Shame."

"I'll cut off your bits if you harm mundanes." Wrenn swung the sword around.

Ranger laughed. He pressed up on the branch and dismounted as beautifully as an Olympic gymnast. "There's lakes here, luv." He sniffed the air. "*Sooo mannnyyy* lakes." He shaded his eyes again as he watched the beams of light grow brighter. "If I were ye, I'd be more worried about walkin' intae elf territory wi' a stolen blade." He waved his hand at Red.

If anything, the elves would likely be happy to have it back.

Or not.

Or she might have accidently gotten herself wrapped up in some fae or elf prophecy about swords named Red and inland hurricanes or snownadoes or whatever the local winter hell-weather was.

And she didn't even have a scabbard.

Ranger ran toward the incoming mundanes. "I'm gonnae kill th' three of 'em an' leave ye here wi' th' corpses, sweetheart." He saluted once and ducked under a bush.

The snowmobile in front stopped. The driver dropped his feet and flipped up the visor on his helmet. "You two alright? You drop out of a plane or some—"

Ranger's boot hit the front of the snowmobile. He twisted his hip, swung his other leg, and wrapped it around the man's head.

They smacked into the ground hard enough that a bulging semi-puff of slushy snow welled up around them.

The kelpie was on the snowmobile before she could get close enough to pull him away. "Ranger!" she yelled.

The kelpie saluted again. He looked at one side of the bright yellow overly-decaled vehicle, then the other. Then he turned the snowmobile south.

The second snowmobiler stopped next to his friend still lying in the snow. "Who the hell are you—"

This man's garishly red vehicle carried a cargo box behind the seat. In one twisting movement, Wrenn pulled him off his snowmobile and slammed the sword perpendicularly into the box. Red stuck out of the box like Excalibur from the stone.

"Da *hell*, lady!" the owner of the red vehicle yelled.

The emerald magic around the hilt wove itself down the blade, crisscrossing and braiding until it made its own sheath, and then around the cargo box.

At least she wouldn't fall off.

"Stay out of his way." She pointed at the departing Ranger. "He's dangerous."

The only one still on his snowmobile dug around in his jacket as if looking for his phone.

Wrenn glanced at the vehicle's controls. It didn't look all that different from a motorcycle.

She put the snowmobile in gear and chased the kelpie south.

CHAPTER 12

E d Martinez turned off his siren and lights as he approached the parking area at the southern end of the Paul Bunyan State Forest.

The trees had mostly lost their leaves and stood as the towering skeletal framework holding up this part of the world. Northern Minnesota, at least east of Thief River Falls, was a quilt of state and national parks, natural and scientific regions, and land managed by the tribes. The air was fresher up here. Get within half a state of Canada and the world cleaned up nice.

Ed's radio crackled. "Okay, so," Tracy at dispatch continued. "Seems the guy in the kilt and the woman with the big honkin' sword stole two of Brad Anderson's snowmobiles. His son said the two thieves fell out of the sky or somethin' like that."

Magicals did like to make an entrance. Or Brad and his boys were drunk.

"Copy," Ed responded.

Tracy continued: "Suspects are headin' south. Both snowmobiles are Arctic Cats. One red. One yellow."

South meant that if they followed the trails, they would most likely come out in this parking area. Ed rubbed his forehead again. "Which

Brad Anderson?" There were at least ten in the city of Alfheim alone. Some of them were more credible than others.

Because he'd have to spin this, no matter what, with the sword.

"The one who owns the bait shop out on 107," Tracy said.

That particular Brad Anderson was in fact a drunk who loved to yell at tourists. He'd been banned from multiple restaurants and lodges for bellowing Deep State stupidity and ranting about every idiotic conspiracy theory he found on the internet.

His two sons weren't much better.

"Are we sure the Andersons haven't been hitting the pale ale while out destroying nature's wonders?"

"I was thinkin' that too, but Hubbard County got three separate calls from Manny's Lodge patrons sayin' they saw a flash and then somethin' fallin' into the trees," Tracy said.

This was going to take a lot of spin. "Great," Ed said.

"Brad said the sword looked kinda fancy."

A huge fancy sword. A claymore, perhaps? "Any signs, Tracy?"

Tracey knew that "signs" meant overt usage of magic. "Nope. No points either, Sheriff," she answered.

Points, as in pointy ears, so no elves involved.

He turned onto the park's southern access road. "All right. Out." He dug out his cell phone and dialed the Elf King himself, Arne Odinsson.

The call went to voicemail. "We got a situation in Paul Bunyan," Ed said, and hung up.

Magnus Freyrsson's number also went to voicemail. Ed left the same message.

He got through to Lennart Thorsson, an elf who, when he answered, said exactly what Ed was expecting him to say: "We have a fae problem."

"Color me surprised," Ed answered.

Lennart snorted. "Bjorn, Arne, and Magnus are working on it."

No details. Not because the elves held to their rule about no talking about magic over open airwaves, but because they were all so *private.* They shared only what they deemed valuable, which more often than not meant they shared less than what he needed to do his job.

A lot less.

At least Lennart attempted to understand. But he was an elf, and like all magical creatures everywhere, he was constrained by his nature.

It was still annoying.

"Working on what, Lennart?" Ed asked. "I need to know what I'm driving into here."

Lennart paused. "There was a kelpie. Bjorn says it's gone."

Bjorn Thorsson was the elder elf who owned Raven's Gaze Brewery and Pub. He pretty much embodied Thor's man-of-the-people vibe, where Lennart was more artistic and storm-like.

"A frickin' *kelpie?*" Ed said. "The murdering and raping type or the bad-boy boyfriend romance-novel type?" Because every kind of magical came in every possible flavor, and right now, he'd much rather deal with an arrogant Scottish dude with a mouth than some dark fae who was about to take up residence in the local lakes.

"It's gone, Ed. Bjorn was tracking it until it up and disappeared. Which it shouldn't be able to do on its own, by the way. They're powerful, but they can't open portals or gates on their own. There's no trace left."

Great, Ed thought. "We have a guy in a kilt in Paul Bunyan who, according to good old Brad Anderson, fell out of the sky."

Lennart paused. "Which one? There's a lot of Brad Andersons in town."

Now Ed sighed. He was on his way to deal with a kelpie and the one elf he could get on the phone was being coy. "There's also a tall woman dressed in black."

"Oh," Lennart said. "I thought kelpies were all male."

So the woman might also be a kelpie? "They carry swords?"

"Not that I know of," Lennart said.

"One of you going to come out here and zap the kelpies for me?" He turned into the main parking area and pulled up next to Brad

Anderson's truck and trailer. "Axlam brought the wife and kids dinner and I'd like to partake."

Lennart smacked his lips. "A better choice for the evening, Sheriff Martinez. You have been awake too long. You need food and sleep. Go home. Let one of us deal with the interlopers."

"That'd be nice," Ed said. He shouldn't be short with an elf, especially an elf who had disobeyed an order so as to help Ed's daughter, but he really would like to go home. "I can't. State Patrol and Hubbard County got calls. State Patrol's tied up with the last accident out on 34 but they have someone on the way. This is officially a law enforcement issue."

"Not if they are kelpies," Lennart said.

"I'm already here."

"Okay, okay," said Lennart. "You should be safe. Kelpies affect women. They like to argue, though, so do your best to ignore them."

"Will do," Ed answered.

"And stay back,"

"I plan to," Ed said.

"I will check who is available and call you back."

Lennart hung up.

Ed looked at his phone. Damned elves and their dislike of technology.

He looked around the parking area and clicked his radio. "Nothing out of the ordinary yet at the south entrance, Tracy," he said.

A tiny voice in the back of Ed's mind told him to suit up. A ballistic vest would only be valuable if the Andersons were carrying. Which they might be. They had a history of ignoring laws they didn't like.

The Alfheim County Sheriff's Department operated with more resources than the surrounding counties simply because the elves optimized within a standard county budget. Plus his resources, in particular, carried enchantments.

He was driving the cruiser this weekend because his normal department SUV was "in the shop," in the process of getting yet another layer of magical extras. The elves were "adding protections." What, he didn't know. But part of the aftermath of the incident had been stronger anti-vampire magicks. Ten years in Alfheim and the elves were still sticklers about making sure he and his family were safe.

Safety his family would no longer have access to if he took the family back to Texas.

He rubbed his face. He really did need sleep.

Flashlight in hand, he stepped out of his cruiser and opened the trunk. These were kelpies, not vampires, but they were still dark magicals.

He unlocked his shotgun before popping open his specialty safe.

From the outside, it looked like any standard-issue trunk-mounted gun safe, except when the sun hit it just right and the runes became visible—the runes that, like so many of his upgraded enchantments, were added after the incident.

The elves didn't know about his stash of specialty shells, though.

He loaded in his cold iron- and silver-containing fae shells and quickly read through the checklist he'd taped to the inside of the safe: *Don't take or offer food. Don't take or offer favors, boons, or advice. Don't get close enough to allow the fae to touch you.* And most important: *Do not, for any reason, make a deal.*

Specific fae had specific issues, but his list should keep him safe until elven backup arrived.

Rumbling echoed through the trees. Headlight beams appeared.

Snowmobiles approached.

Ed slammed the cruiser's trunk and shouldered the shotgun as he walked toward the head of the trail to await their fae visitors.

CHAPTER 13

W renn Goodfellow tossed up a simple shield spell to minimize the cold wind hitting her face. She didn't have anything anywhere near as powerful as the wedge spell Robin had used to keep them safe from the kelpie stampede, but she could at least keep the snow out of her eyes.

The three mundanes rode their one remaining snowmobile, and even though they fell behind, they hadn't veered off or stopped. They'd catch up sooner or later and cause more problems.

Up ahead a trail sign came into view, pointing southwest toward a parking area. A plume of magic rose off Ranger as he stood on the snowmobile's sideboards and sniffed the air slamming into his face. Then he spun the vehicle around a tree and took off down the signed trail.

Ranger looked over his shoulder, saluted, and sped toward the waiting cars.

He was going to steal a new vehicle. But why? She was pretty sure elves were going to show up any minute now.

Over her two centuries, she'd had only one decidedly unpleasant interaction with an elf, a French male descended from the enclave established alongside the Norse colony that became Normandy.

They'd crossed paths in Paris. He'd been nonchalant about pretty much everything, not caring about fae, or vampires, or other elves. Mostly he'd been just another pretty male doing boring, subversively violent, pretty male things.

Her hopes really weren't much higher for American elves. Especially American elves who harbored not only vampires, but also Victor's first monster.

The American over-inflated sense of entitlement meant they thought they could make anyone and everyone do what they wanted. Such grandiose foolishness was annoying when mundanes did it and outright dangerous when magicals were involved.

Still, she didn't have the magic to return a kelpie to Oberon's Castle. She'd need to get Ranger to the gate at the tavern. Or worse—she'd need elven help.

But what would help from these particular elves mean? The fact that she was carrying one of their swords was probably going to set off a major political tiff between the enclaves and King Oberon no matter how Wrenn handled the situation. And then there was the question of Victor's creation.

Would they allow her near the monster? They'd protected vampires. Were they protecting a creature just as evil? Why?

This might be her only chance to find answers.

Yet she couldn't let Ranger get away. The threat of a kelpie-vampire alliance and a blood syndicate moving magical blood far outweighed any personal need on her part.

She bumped along the frozen ground and followed Ranger onto the trail. They rounded a curve into an open area—and right into the blinding beam of a military-grade flashlight shining from a parking lot a good twenty feet away.

A flashlight held by a mundane against the barrel of a shotgun. "Alfheim County Sheriff!" he shouted. "Turn off the snowmobiles and put your hands in the air! *Now!*"

Ranger pulled his vehicle around so it faced the lawman and turned it off. He did not raise his hands.

Wrenn pulled up parallel to the kelpie, but far enough away he couldn't jump her and roll her off the snowmobile.

Ranger pointed at the officer. "Will ye look at that!" he called. "They sent their pet *sheriff* t' take care o' *us!*"

The officer kept the light mostly on Ranger. "Identify yourselves." He leaned his head to the side and said something into his shoulder-mounted radio.

"Now, now, laddie, yer gonnae need t' do better than that," Ranger crooned. He didn't seem one bit concerned about the shotgun.

Wrenn didn't have a lot of experience with guns. They were close to useless when dealing with vampires and fae unless they were specially modified and took specially enchanted ammunition.

You had to get up and personal when dealing with the darkness of the universe.

No overt magic wafted off the officer, so he wasn't carrying any specific, strong enchantments. If the elves had granted him smaller magicks, she couldn't see them through the glare of his light. "My name is Wrenn Goodfellow," she said. "I'm…" How to identify herself in a way that would make sense to someone who knew about magic, but would mean nothing to a regular mundane? "I'm also… law enforcement… where we come from."

Hopefully, the pauses would get across what she needed to communicate.

The officer said something about "needing points out here" into his radio.

Points? Was that a reference to the pointy ears of elves? "I'm assuming you understand what… law enforcement… means?" Wrenn asked.

"Yes," said the officer.

Ranger sniffed at the air again. "How many elves did ye call in, little man?" He sniffed again. "The reek o' these infernal hell-beasts," he slapped the handlebars of his snowmobile, "is keepin' me from countin'." He leaned toward Wrenn. "Gotta catch 'em all, ye know, sweetling."

He winked.

The three mundanes roared into the clearing. They buzzed their snowmobile back and forth across the head of the trail a few times before stopping.

The driver flipped up the mask of his helmet. "Those are my snowmobiles, Sheriff!" he yelled.

"I know, Brad Anderson," the officer responded. "Now give these two a wide berth and come around to the parking lot."

One of the passengers pointed at Wrenn. "She stuck her fancy-ass sword through my cargo case!"

"So give her a wide berth and come around to the parking lot, will ya?" the officer said.

The same kid pointed at Ranger. "That one headlocked Dad with his thighs and he's got nothing on under that skirt of his!"

Ranger chuckled.

The flashlight beam landed squarely on Ranger. "Let the man talk."

Ranger shrugged and smoothed the front of his polo shirt. "It's brisk here!" He looked over his shoulder directly at the three mundanes. "Best if we all went in t' warm up wi' some whiskey, eh, boys? Talk about th' local lassies, aye?"

An enthrallment wave washed off his kelpie body.

He couldn't affect men. Or could he? The vamped kelpie in the tavern had enthralled everyone, male and female. But Ranger wasn't a vampire.

Wrenn swung her leg over her snowmobile. The sword hadn't talked to her, or glowed, or done anything at all since she'd thrust it into the case. The emerald magic around its hilt had dimmed down to nothing more than a faint shimmer, too.

She pulled it out and pointed it at Ranger.

"Hey!" the one the officer had called Brad Anderson yelled. "You let him be!"

Ranger had definitely affected the men.

The kelpie snickered. "Hey, officer! This woman is gonnae manhandle me!"

The officer did not move from his location on the edge of the lot. "I can see that," he said.

Ranger frowned as if he'd expected the officer to be as affected as the three on the snowmobile. "That's disappointin'."

Brad Anderson revved his snowmobile. "Unhand him, harpy, or Brad Jr. and Connor here will have words with you!"

"Unhand him, harpy?" the officer said, and aimed his shotgun. "What'd you do to them?"

Ranger smiled. "Bradley, Bradley Jr., an' Connor. *Hmmm...*"

It couldn't be their Scottish names that allowed the enthralling. Magic didn't work that way.

Ranger rolled his eyes. "It's easy t' trigger aggression in like-minded men."

Wrenn was well-aware of like-minded men. Victor had been a like-minded man.

The officer briefly threw the beam of his light onto the mundanes. "You Anderson boys turn off your snowmobile. Now!"

The driver turned off the engine. "This is all because they hired *one of you*," he said.

Disdain dripped off *one of you*.

"We aren't going to start with that, now are we, Brad Anderson?" the officer called.

The two boys got off the back and stepped away from the snowmobile.

Another wave of enthralling rolled off Ranger.

If she didn't get this under control, the kelpie would get these mundanes to kill each other before any elf showed up. So Wrenn did the only thing she could think of that might make a real difference: She reached for the braided leather around Ranger's neck.

Ranger pushed his near shoulder toward Wrenn's body and lowered a hand to grab for the wrist of her sword hand.

He twisted. Her free hand flew by his neck.

Ranger grabbed both her wrists, one in each hand, and held her arms out, locked into position and unable to use the sword or throw up a protection spell.

She should be able to overpower him. He hadn't been vamped. He was strong—all kelpies were strong—but she'd been chosen as a paladin because very few fae could physically match her strength. Yet she couldn't move.

She yanked. His biceps under the cuffs of his polo shirt bulged. But he held on.

Ranger pushed his face directly into her breasts. "Why is it ye can ignore me, lass?" he crooned.

Waves of shock rolled through Wrenn. He nuzzled and rubbed and murmured but didn't harm. But he *was* harming. He held her hands. And—

Behind them, the Andersons laughed.

"Let. Go. Ranger!" Wrenn yelled directly into his ear.

Ranger chuckled as he rubbed his face against her chest again.

"Let go of the lady, *Ranger*," the officer called.

Ranger pulled his face out long enough to wink up at Wrenn. "Ye've nae say in this, little man," he growled.

The officer primed his gun. "Yes, I do."

Ranger's grip tightened to the point it hurt. "Oh, lassie—" He blinked and rolled her wrist without the sword so he could see the inside. "A token." He looked up at her. "Because ye're a witch, eh?"

What difference did her Heartway tokens make? "This will not end well for you," Wrenn growled.

Ranger chuckled. "It's cute ye think there's an alternative." He nodded toward the officer.

She leaned her head down. "You answer my questions and I will ask the King for lenience."

He lifted his head. "Ye hear that, lads? The King's gonnae go easy on dear ol' me!" He laughed. "I'm here because o' *my* King."

His King? "Our Kings are the same king."

His eyebrows arched and he loosened his grip slightly. Not enough to get away, but enough to indicate he was listening. "D'ye really think we dinnae have our own *king*? Tsk. Tsk."

"Roll back your enthralling on these boys so we can discuss this like adults," Wrenn said.

"Oh, luv, I only worry about th' ones wi' th' downward points," He curled his lip.

Vampires.

The officer's radio buzzed. "Copy that," the officer said. He flicked the light toward the Andersons. "I want you boys to sit down on the snow. Drop your asses right where you are and test out the quality of those suits you're wearing. Got it?"

None of them moved.

Ranger blinked. His brow contorted again, and he peered at the officer. Then he looked back at the Andersons. "They said *one o' ye* like he's some kind of invader or somethin', didnae they?"

"Let go of me, Ranger," Wrenn said.

He shook his head. "What's yer name, sir?" he called.

"Alfheim County Sheriff's Department," the officer said.

One of the Andersons pointed at the officer again. "That there is Ed-*whar*-do Mar-*tine*-ez," he snarled out, giving extra emphasis on the syllables that must have sounded the most Spanish to their Anderson ears.

Ranger's eyes and mouth rounded. "Well, hot damn, my friend!" He pushed Wrenn away without trying to strip the sword. "Ye're famous all along the *Gulf Coast.*"

The American vampires knew this man.

She should skewer Ranger right here and now. Just run him through, disrupt the enthralling, and keep him from harming the mundanes.

But she needed answers. She still didn't know what the kelpies had tried to steal, or anything at all about the blood syndicate.

"Magnus *Freyr*sson just brought home a couple Australian kelpies." More than a hint of Texas drawl infused the officer's accent. "I wonder if one of them's named Ranger."

He emphasized the Freyr part. They must have an elder Freyr elf in this enclave. Ranger was about to get his ass kicked, for sure.

One of the Anderson boys pointed. "Your pop's gave you a dog name, dude!"

Ranger's eyes narrowed.

"And here I thought your name was Dumbass McHorseface," the officer said.

84

Ranger had hit a nerve with his mention of the Gulf Coast vamps. A nerve that put Officer Martinez on an even more precarious edge.

"I think you should return to your vehicle, Sheriff, and allow me to handle Ranger," she said.

He tipped his head to the side as if to remind her about the strength of Ranger's grip.

"Yeah!" one of the Andersons yelled. "How'd some damned illegal get a job as sheriff anyway? *I* didn't vote for ya!"

"Yeah!" another yelled. "How'd you rig the election, huh?"

Sheriff Martinez pointed the light right at Father Anderson's face. "Sit. Your ass. *Down!*"

Ranger's lip curled. Red demon flame leaked from the sides of his eyes as he stared at the Sheriff. His muscles tensed.

He was going to attack Martinez. His body language screamed his intention so loudly the mundanes all shifted as if they'd noticed.

He might have blinked before he lunged. Maybe. He might have yelled, or sworn in Scottish, or done any of the other flamboyant things she'd come to expect from a kelpie.

But something was clear: He'd decided that the Sheriff was more valuable than enthralling the Andersons, or egging on Wrenn, or even his mysterious reasons for attacking the Gallery.

And he was instantly outside of strike range and well within Martinez's blast range.

"Don't!" Wrenn yelled.

Don't shoot the kelpie, she thought. *Don't make him more frightened than he already is.*

Because fear was the root of his behavior. All the anger, all the posturing, all the evil behavior rose out of *terror*. It did with all the fae. It did with everyone, even her.

The blast hit Ranger directly in the chest.

And she couldn't stop him if the terror overwhelmed his nasty kelpie mind.

He gulped and looked down at the hole in his polo shirt. He snarled. Then he dropped to his knees. "Cold iron *an'* silver. I think I love ye so much I'm gonnae tell my friends where t' find ye, *Santo Guijarro County Deputy* Eduardo Martinez."

Ranger was a kelpie. He shouldn't know anything about this man's past. Which meant the Gulf Coast clans had a bounty out on the elves' sheriff—and that Ranger had enough connections to the clan to pick up this particular bit of information. There was no other explanation.

That vamped kelpie hadn't been an anomaly, like Robin had suggested. Dark fae—kelpies—*were* trafficking for a blood syndicate. Ranger and his big mouth were her proof.

And Ranger threatening a mundane law enforcement officer in elf territory made this entire situation a thousand times worse than she'd thought.

Sheriff Martinez primed his shotgun again.

"Don't!" Wrenn swished the sword in the Andersons' direction. "You! On your knees."

"Like we'd listen to *you*," one spat.

"I will arrest all three of you boys," Sheriff Martinez called.

Father Anderson climbed back onto the snowmobile. "We'll go find that fine wife of yours," he snarled.

"*Yesssss*," Ranger hissed. He sniffed the air. "An' bairns, too. Tasty." He ran two fingers of one hand through the blood on his chest, then two fingers of the other.

He jumped up to standing, arms wide and shoulders tense.

Martinez aimed the shotgun. "I need backup out here *now!*" he yelled into his radio.

Ranger made a kissy face at the Sheriff. Then he turned toward the Andersons. "Lads." He ran his bloody fingers across his cheekbones, leaving two red stripes on either side of his face. "Shall we?"

CHAPTER 14

The sun set behind the tress, spreading black lines of shadow over the crispy snow. Birds chirped. In the distance, car engines roared.

Halfway between Wrenn and Sheriff Martinez, Ranger snarled. His pale green eyes shimmered with his dark fae power. And his enthralled minions hyperventilated and frothed at the mouth.

The Sheriff held rock steady with his shotgun pointed at Ranger's head.

Wrenn didn't think he'd ever killed a magical before, at least not with a gun, and not in a situation like this. Not when it was such a threat of magical malevolence.

Ranger would kill the man's wife and daughters. Of this Wrenn had no doubt. If Ranger left the small area between the trees and the parking lot, he'd leave behind a trail of dead women—the Sheriff's family, the Andersons' family, any low-powered elf he could find—anyone. Even Wrenn.

Because something had changed. Something about landing in elf territory had made him stronger.

Wrenn stabbed the sword into the engine block of Ranger's snowmobile. It slid in as if cutting through butter and with only the tiniest of metal-on-metal shrieks.

"Ye think that will stop me?" Ranger bellowed. "I can run faster than that thing can plow through the underbrush."

But it would keep his mundane mob here. Wrenn sliced the engine block of her snowmobile.

Father Anderson screeched like a toddler. "Those are *mine!*" he whined.

His boys danced around and threw their helmets at the trees, but all three took up position between Ranger and Wrenn and the remaining snowmobile.

Ranger rubbed his forehead. "Fine, darlin'. We'll do this th' hard—"

A bolt of magic hit Ranger dead center on his shoulder joint. A second one hit Wrenn on hers. Both bolts brightened to blinding as they exploded outward from their impact sites like little mushroom clouds.

The one that hit Ranger rose off the fabric of his polo as he twisted to look at the impact point.

That mushroom cap of magic slammed down and spread over his body like a glass cocoon.

Wrenn tried to turn toward the source of the magic. She tried. She got her body twisted enough that she faced the Sheriff before her little mushroom of magic exploded too.

She couldn't move. She breathed fine, at least for the moment, but the sheen of magic over her entire body held her like a statue.

"I'm law enforcement!" she tried to call, but only a whisper came out.

Never in her life had Wrenn seen such a strong containment spell, and never had she seen one so precise.

The flashlight cut out.

Wrenn blinked against the gloom as the whole clearing dropped into twilight.

Another, softer spell flashed by, presumably headed for the Andersons.

"You boys leave your Cats, got it?" said a new, melodic, beautifully feminine voice. "Go sit at the picnic table over there." A hand moved through the shadow. "You found your snowmobiles damaged, understand? The thieves got away."

"*Ahh...*" said Father Anderson.

The voice spoke again. "You tell the State Troopers you saw nothing."

"We saw nothing," the two boys said in unison.

Wrenn squinted, trying to see through the gloom. A wall of magic stood about five feet in front of the Sheriff, between him and Ranger specifically, making it even more difficult to make out details.

Next to Sheriff Martinez, encased in wave after wave of aurora borealis-colored magic, was an elf woman. She wore a puffy pink winter jacket and a floppy-brimmed hat, one meant to hide the tall points of her ears. Her massive black elven ponytail cascaded out from the back of the hat and swayed almost as if it was as alive as the elf. She was slightly shorter than Wrenn, just under six feet tall.

"Sheriff Martinez," the elf said.

"Benta," he said. "I appreciate you driving all the way out here."

She'd glamoured down her radiance, but not a lot. Just enough to fool the idiot mundanes gawking at her from around their snowmobile.

She shimmered like an angel. A real, extraordinarily beautiful angel.

"She's an elder elf," Ranger whispered through his containment spell. He sniffed like a dog. "An aspect of frickin' *Freya*, for th' love o' th' Four Kings. She's gonnae *kill* me an' feed my horse corpse t' her cats." He cooed out a sigh. "An' I'd happily let her."

"Better fate than you deserve," Wrenn said. What had he said? What four kelpie kings? That was not a story she'd heard. "Four Kings, Ranger?"

A low growl made it through his containment spell. "She's gonnae kill ye too, fer havin' tha' pretty hors d'oeuvres picker."

The elf didn't appear angry enough to kill anyone. But then again, elves weren't fae. If this elf determined that Wrenn was as much of a threat as Ranger, she might kill Wrenn in order to save her community any trouble. Or so Robin had told Wrenn many times.

"I apologize for not getting here sooner," the elf named Benta said. "The roads are a mess, as you know."

Sheriff Martinez *hmphed*.

"You Anderson boys move on over to the picnic bench. Go on." Benta snapped her fingers and pointed.

Behind Wrenn, the Andersons all inhaled and shuffled through the snow toward the bench.

"I believe it might be time for our King to have words with the more problematic of the local mundanes," Benta said.

Sheriff Martinez snorted.

"They're busy, Ed." She looked him up and down. "You should not be out here alone."

"You think?" He pointed at Ranger. "There's something bigger happening here."

Benta frowned. "There is," she says. "We deal with these two first."

"That one says she's fae law enforcement." Sheriff Martinez waved his hand toward Wrenn.

The elf named Benta unzipped her coat as she walked toward the snowmobiles. "Fae laws? *Ha*." She revealed a perfect hourglass dressed only in a crop top under the coat.

"*Damn*," Ranger breathed. "I'm in *love*."

Elven tattoos circled the elf's waist. She flicked her wrists again.

The magic on her fingertips danced onto her tattoos. Colors rose. Patterns formed. And a new sigil hit Ranger.

"He's a kelpie, alright," she said. "And thankfully not something worse masquerading as a pretty-boy horse." She walked toward Ranger. "Kelpies are not welcome in Alfheim."

"It's nae my fault," he whispered through his containment spell, and did his best to nod toward Wrenn.

Benta turned to Wrenn. "You claim to be law enforcement?"

"I am," Wrenn whispered.

A new sigil formed around Benta's fingers. She slapped it against Wrenn's chest.

Fire screamed up Wrenn's throat. She gasped, but it disappeared as fast as it hit.

"You're carrying some complicated fae magicks." Benta stepped back. Her eyes narrowed. She leaned her head back to call to Sheriff Martinez but kept her eyes on Wrenn. "She's *not* fae. I can't get a good read because of the enchantments." She leaned closer again. "*Huh*. Ed, please come here."

"I'm a Royal Guard Paladin," Wrenn whispered. "I hunt vampires and dark fae for the King. I'm on a case." Dare she say more to the elf? She needed to understand the politics here first. If she pissed off the elves, she might inadvertently get herself in trouble with the King. Worse, she could cause an incident.

Benta stepped back. "Oberon." A string of Old Norse followed.

Or cause a war.

"Wrong thing t' say t' an elf, darlin'," Ranger whispered.

"Quiet." Benta slapped a secondary spell over his mouth.

"Please release me so I can return the kelpie to Oberon's Castle. We will deal with him there," Wrenn said.

Sheriff Martinez watched Ranger more than Wrenn or the elf, and still held his shotgun ready. He walked over and stood behind Benta.

The elder elf stepped closer and tilted her head to the side as she peered at Wrenn's eyes. Then she stepped to the side as if looking for marks or scars along Wrenn's hairline. "Ed," she said. "There's a resemblance here, is there not?"

The Sheriff gave Wrenn the first good look all evening. His eyebrows arched. "You got family here, Ms. Law Enforcement?"

Family. "No," she said. The "family" she had here was not her *family*. Not at all.

He shrugged. "What about the sword?"

"I got it by accident," Wrenn said.

Benta frowned. "There are no accidents with the fae." She peered at the sword. "Woodland sharks, the lot of them."

Not Robin. Well, yes Robin, but at least Robin had some scruples.

Benta reached for the sword. "What's your name, mundane?"

She wasn't a mundane. She was a witch. Better, though, that the elf thought her a mundane. "Wrenn," she said. "Wrenn Goodfellow."

Benta snatched back her hand. "*Goodfellow?* And you carry an elven blade?"

Ranger's eyes widened and he smirked as if to say *Ye've stepped in it now, luv.*

Sheriff Martinez leaned toward Benta. "If she really hunts vampires, maybe she can tell us why the kelpie *knows.*"

He was referring to the Gulf Coast vamps. "I'd like to know, too," Wrenn said. "I think it's caught up in my case."

Officer Martinez pointed at Wrenn. "I want to talk to this one."

Benta shook her head. "No deals, Ed. Not even with fae-adjacent mundanes."

He scowled.

The elf's wrists flicked. Two small, tight, fast-spinning sigils formed at her fingertips.

She grabbed for the sword still in Wrenn's grip.

And the huge fancy elven blade, the one that had maybe told Wrenn its name was Red, the one she felt might be a *she*—the one that was otherwise just a sword—decided it had an opinion.

Mine! exploded off the sword as a concussive wave.

A wave of blue-white, electrical magic.

CHAPTER 15

T he elf named Benta took the blast full in the face and yet somehow stood her ground. Sheriff Martinez fell over into the snow. And Wrenn...

This was not the first time in Wrenn's life she'd stood in the center of a ball of possessiveness. She'd watched possessiveness take on the shape of blindingly blue-white light before.

The moment when Victor's vampire creation had ripped Victor's head from his body—the memory, the vision, the pain and terror and screaming—overlaid itself over reality as if the moment itself was the true fiend.

And for a split second—less than a split second, or maybe more, maybe a whole lifetime—the sword in Wrenn's hand became Victor's lightning rod. The possessiveness became Victor. The Sheriff fell to the ground and out of the intruding overlay of her memories ... but Ranger did not.

Ranger did what all kelpies do—he flared his nostrils and pulled in the scent of her frozen muscles and her thumping heart. And Ranger became the monster.

But he had always been a monster. Like Victor's, a beautiful one, but with pale green eyes. An inordinately perfect specimen of male size, shape, terror, and rage.

And the real-world wave of possessiveness that had burst off the sword, the wave that had knocked her memories back into her vision, the ball of magic from the elven blade did something much worse than knocking the sheriff to the ground.

It stripped the containment spells off Wrenn and Ranger.

He was free to rip the head off the world.

The sword had no idea what it had done. It had barked at the elf and gone back to sleep like some giant narcoleptic war dog.

It was still in Wrenn's hand. Still heavy and superbly balanced and sharp as death itself. Still something that, like Victor, was probably going to haunt her for the rest of her life.

Her fingers spasmed. Her forearm jerked.

Wrenn dropped the elven sword.

Ranger twisted his shoulder and swept his hand toward the hilt. He arched and he lunged and he grabbed the hilt just before he landed on his back in the snow.

The blue-white memory overlay popped and sparked as if the screen on which Wrenn's brain projected it burned. All that remained were embers in the corners of her vision.

Ranger grinned up at her where he lay in the snow, arm up and hand around the hilt of her sword in a reverse grip. "Aye, she's more claymore than Viking toothpicker, ain't she?"

He was right there, right in front of her, on the ground, grinning up at her with red demon fire escaping from the sides of his eyes, holding her sword in such a way as to make it harder for him to attack than if he just dropped it.

She pulled back her foot and let Ranger catch the full brunt of the fae steel in the tip of her boot.

He rolled with the kick but she managed to open a gash along his cheek.

"I am fully within my rights as Royal Guard here, Ranger." She kicked at the shoulder of the arm that held her sword, but he rolled again. "I can and will kill you for being an eminent threat to mundanes and any treaties King Oberon has with these elves."

Information on the blood syndicate be damned.

There were other kelpies involved. Two others had come through the dryads' portal. Robin was probably interrogating them right now in the comfort of the castle.

Not in the snow and cold. Not in the twilight between day and night in the mundane world. Not with a beautiful but stunned elf who stood perfectly still and blinking as if she didn't remember where she was.

The Sheriff pulled himself to standing. He favored a hip, but had his shotgun back at his shoulder before Wrenn came in for her third kick to Ranger's head. "Benta?" He looked her over.

When she didn't respond, he aimed the shotgun at Ranger's face. "The shells make you bleed. This close to your face I'll probably blind you," he said.

Wrenn aimed her next kick at Ranger's crotch.

Ranger drove the point of the sword into the ground and raised his free hand. "Wait!" He braced himself with the blade, and now had leverage, even if he still held the hilt in a reverse grip.

Wrenn held her kick. "Move away from the sword."

He looked at his fist and the sword, back up to her, then at the end of the shotgun barrel. "I'm needin' a deal here," he said.

The Sheriff poked the gun at Ranger. "No deals!"

"I'm *a lot* faster than ye, little mundane," Ranger snarled.

He kept glancing at the elf.

The moment she came out of her stupor, she'd kill him. She might even kill Wrenn, for having a sword capable of overpowering an elder elf.

"Why did you break into the Gallery of Artifacts?" Wrenn asked.

Ranger didn't remove his hand from the sword's hilt. "Bridles, ye ignorant tart." The red flames around his eyes flared.

Bridles? In the Gallery?

"*Whose* bridles?" For the first time in her years as a paladin, Wrenn wished she'd been trained on firearms. "Sheriff Martinez here could easily blow off your nose."

"Oh *oh oh*!" Ranger said. "So th' bonny elves saved yer ass, an' made ye th' actual honest-to-all-their-silly-gods head o' policin' in their territory?" He guffawed. "A *mundane*?"

"Are all kelpies like this?" Sheriff Martinez asked.

Wrenn nodded. "This one's not special."

Ranger pointed at the Sheriff. "Though he *is* a special mundane. He killed a granddaddy Gulf Coast vamp wi' his *bare hands*."

Martinez groaned. "Shut. Up."

Ranger chuckled. "They would *looooovvvvveeee* t' get their spindly spider fingers on *ye*." He sniffed. "Or one o' those…." He sniffed again. "Four?" Another sniff. "Five spawn o' yers? Ye've been a busy man, my friend."

In one swift, perfect movement, Ranger planted his feet and used his grip on the sword to push himself to standing.

Martinez primed the gun. "Benta! Now would be a good time for you to wake up!"

But Ranger didn't pull the sword from the frozen ground. He stared at the elf. "I meant it, wi' th' deal."

"You're a liar," Wrenn said.

Ranger laughed. "Ye're a quick learner, darlin'." He flipped his grip on the sword so that he'd be holding it correctly if he pulled it from the ground. "Deals." He shook his head. "We were fine till all those vampires disappeared last month."

The Sheriff poked the gun at him again. "What are you talking about?"

Benta stirred.

Ranger pointed his chin at her. "What happens when th' enclaves get their hierarchies in a twist?" Then he pointed it at Wrenn. "Or us, sweets? What happens when th' elders an' th' powerful smell a vacancy?"

Martinez swore.

Ranger nodded toward him. "*He* understands." He tapped the middle of his forehead. "We can only trust our own." He sniffed again.

"An' wi' *my* kind, that doesnae work, either." He shrugged. "We do stupid things."

"You were running victims to the vampires." This she'd already figured out. "But those vamps vanished? Died?" She only knew something had changed.

"Vanished," Martinez said.

Ranger nodded knowingly. "See? He understands."

"But the ones left still wanted their fill, didn't they?" Wrenn asked. Started feeding on—and turned at least one of—their victim-running kelpies when their power structure was disrupted.

Because vampires could never be trusted.

Ranger sighed. "Oh, they wanted a lot more than their fill."

"Did they want extra magicals?" she asked. How else were they to get just that extra bit of specialness needed to become the Big Vampire in Town? "They turned on you." Looks like eleven exsanguinated sprites wasn't enough.

Ranger yanked out the sword and took three steps backward. "O' course they turned on us. That doesnae mean I cannae bring them..." He looked directly at Sheriff Martinez. "... a peace offerin'."

What had been a man in a black polo shirt and a black tactical kilt became the draft-horse-sized stallion she'd met in the castle.

"Benta!" the Sheriff shouted.

The sword floated just off the shimmering pale-green hide on his back, making it far enough up she'd have a hard time grabbing it.

His bridle also lifted off his hide. It flared out with a sweet tinkling sound, and coiled down his horse neck and his horse back.

Ranger made himself a scabbard to carry her sword.

"*Kelpie!*"

Benta flipped off her jacket as she unfroze. Every single tattoo on her waist glowed. She ripped off the hat and all the tattoos along her hairline popped out white-hot like a crown.

She rolled up a crackling, almost-ultraviolet ball of magic and whipped it at Ranger's head.

The ball grazed the Sheriff as it flew by. He swore and spun toward Wrenn, clearly somehow affected.

She caught him before he fell and he just as quickly rolled out of her grasp.

"No worries," she said.

He frowned, then nodded toward Ranger and the elf.

Ranger had dodged the ball of magic. He bolted into the trees.

Instead of checking on the Sheriff, or Wrenn, Benta the elder elf ran after the kelpie.

CHAPTER 16

"I have two daughters." Martinez rubbed at the spot where the elf's magic had grazed his shoulder. "Third is due in two weeks."

His wife was about to have a baby. A girl.

Would Ranger really go after the Sheriff's family? "Do you live in town or on a body of water?" Wrenn asked.

"Around here it's pretty much all trees and bodies of water." He stumbled toward his cruiser. "You coming?" he called. Then into his radio: "Tracy, call Gerard. Tell him I need whoever's awake to head to my place."

The radio crackled. "Copy," Tracy said.

He peered at the Andersons sitting at the picnic table. They were chatting amongst themselves, telling snowmobile stories or some such nonsense, and were completely ignoring the fuss around them.

"At least that spell held." He nodded toward the trees. "What did that kelpie do to her? I didn't think they were powerful enough to harm an elder elf."

So the sword yelling *Mine!* hadn't been real-world audible. "It wasn't the kelpie," Wrenn said.

Sheriff Martinez stopped between her and his police cruiser.

"What'd *you* do, then?" He flipped the shotgun in his hand to have a better grip if he needed to aim quickly.

"The sword released a wave of hot magic when she tried to take it from me," Wrenn said. "Its name is Red. It's a she. It's talking to me. Maybe. Not in words, except for the whole yelling *Mine!* when Benta reached for her."

Eduardo Martinez, the Sheriff entrusted by elves to watch over their mundanes, cocked one eyebrow, inhaled deeply, and released a dad-worthy sigh unlike any Wrenn had heard before. "You have a big sword named Red that gets jealous anytime someone tries to take her away from you?" He sounded as if he'd heard all this before.

"I wouldn't say she's my sword. I grabbed her because she was the closest weapon."

He nodded in the way all fathers nodded while listening to a child explain how the kitten in the kitchen had found the child and not the other way around. *It was destiny, Papa. Fate. Of course we have to take care of it. Odin said so.*

He sighed again, but not into the dismissive father stance as if he'd made up his mind about adopting a new kitty. No, his stance dropped fully into detective. "No family here, huh? You sure?" He watched her face and shoulders as if looking more for body language clues explaining why she kept denying the obvious.

"No family."

"*Hmmm…*" He pointed at the Royal Guard star on her belt as he pulled out his cell phone. "What's that mean?"

Wrenn unclipped the star. The champagne gold and silver metal weighed enough that her hip always felt its addition or subtraction. "I am a Royal Guard Paladin of King Oberon of the Fae." Which meant nothing here. Not in elf country.

"Paladin for a king." He did the same scoff-snort and eyebrow lift he'd done earlier as he pointed at the cruiser. "Protocol says you ride in the back." He tapped at the phone and held it to his ear.

She clipped the star back onto her belt. "Ranger is part of a bigger investigation. My job is to bring him home," she said. "I'm not going to harm you, Sheriff Martinez."

He peered at her again then looked away when someone answered. "We have an issue," he said into the phone. "I'm calling Lennart and Bjorn. They'll be on their way. I want you to get your sisters and your mom and go into the room in the basement, okay? And call Axlam. Tell her where you are in the house."

He must be talking to his son.

"I'm on my way." He cut the call.

After a moment, he nodded once and pointed at the cruiser. "Go around to the passenger side," he said.

Wrenn jogged around and wedged herself into the passenger seat between the computer rack and door. At least he kept his car clean and she wasn't sitting on his half-eaten lunch.

Martinez dropped into the driver's seat. The dome light illuminated the entire interior of the cruiser, giving Wrenn a good look not only at many gadgets of modern mundane law enforcement, but also his features.

He was shorter than her by about three inches, which made him average height for a mundane man. A five-o'clock shadow accentuated the strong angles of his jaw. He wore a bark-brown Alfheim County Sheriff jacket and a beanie from under which no hair escaped, so she assumed he wore the same short cut pretty much every mundane male cop everywhere had.

He made another call as she strapped in. A few taps and he held it up to his ear. "Benta's chasing the kelpie. He stole the big fancy sword and is in stallion form." He started up the cruiser. "He threatened my family, Lennart."

"We're on our way," the other person said.

The call disconnected.

Martinez pulled the cruiser around, phone still in his hand, and headed for the park's entrance. "Do fae hang up like that?" he asked.

"Oh, yes." Wrenn shrugged. "Magic operates better face to face."

He hit a button and the cruiser's blue and red lights came on.

Wrenn pinched her eyes closed and rubbed her forehead. Flashing lights never bothered her. *Light* didn't bother her, and now all of a sudden she'd had two episodes in one twenty-four-hour period.

"Are you sensitive to lights?"

When she looked up, he was pointing at the roof of the cruiser.

"No…" She sat up straight. "Not usually."

He turned out onto a two-lane road. "Okay," he said. He glanced at her. "We're going to communicate here. Law enforcement to law enforcement. Got it?"

She nodded.

"Ranger was with you prior to falling out of the sky into the park?"

"Yes," she said.

"So he wasn't the kelpie the elves were chasing earlier." He hit the siren and the accelerator. "You two are a brand-new fae problem."

So the elves were in the middle of another "fae problem," which Wrenn guessed probably had something to do with the Queen.

And the Queen was the reason Ranger had gotten into the castle in the first place.

"All of which is tangential to our kelpie-vampire problem," she said.

"Nothing any magical ever does is tangential," he said. "*Nothing.*" He turned onto another, wider road. "More likely we're dealing with multiple overlapping world-ending scenarios here."

He was correct, of course. Most magicals were the volatile centers of their own universes, and when those universes collided, worlds often did end.

"True," she answered.

"So we deal with them one at a time." The look he threw her said *I dare you to argue.*

"There is an imminent threat to your family," Wrenn said.

He nodded, clearly satisfied with her answer. "I killed a vampire back in Texas." He pointed at his neck. "Got a scar to prove it. I thought I was dealing with a mundane serial killer. The Alfheim Pack thought they were dealing with a crazy werewolf, which is why when they showed up, they had two elves in tow." They hit a bumpy patch of ice, and he slowed the cruiser. "I didn't learn the vamp was affiliated with the Gulf Coast clans until after."

Ranger had made it sound as if the Gulf Coast clans didn't know where Martinez and his family lived.

Then again, she'd had no idea that Victor's first creation lived here, either. "The elves are good at keeping their business private, aren't they?" she asked.

He glanced at her again. "Seems so."

"Yet they kept two vampires in town until recently," she said.

He threw her a surprised look.

"The Royal Guard got a copy of the video of the little elf girl."

The surprise turned to fear. Then it vanished. His detective face reemerged.

"Law enforcement to law enforcement," she said.

He nodded. "I'm not privy to most of the magicks around here. The elves, as you say, are private."

She nodded. "Most of the workings of Oberon's Castle are above my pay grade."

Martinez grinned. Wrenn grinned back.

"How do I kill a kelpie?" he asked.

Wrenn chuckled. "You point at the kelpie and ask nicely for the nearest magical to take care of the problem."

"*Heh,*" he said.

"I'm a witch," she said. "I can protect myself, but that's about it. I'm nowhere near powerful enough to bring Ranger to heel." She inhaled. "He's stronger than most kelpies, so be aware."

He nodded. "Witch, huh?"

"Don't know what my ancestry is, though I likely carry elven blood. I was born in Scotland."

Buildings appeared up ahead along with signs warning of a decreased speed limit.

"Welcome to Alfheim, Minnesota," Martinez said as they passed a big wooden sign carved with the same words.

He looked her up and down as he turned down a city street. "When we have this under control, I'm going ask you a few questions about Scotland," he said.

She nodded.

"Now we focus."

She nodded again.

He turned another corner.

And all hell broke loose.

CHAPTER 17

The Martinez home...

Gabriel was the only Martinez child not born in elf territory. He'd been a toddler when they'd moved, a baby really, and he had no memory of Texas. He carried no real concept of dry desert air, or sunsets in colors other than pink and gold. And even though he'd visited many parts of the state of Minnesota, he'd only once been farther south than Des Moines, Iowa.

He remembered the arguments. Could they take the kids to Disney World? *No. We can't. We don't dare.* How about Disneyland? *Do you know how many favors I'll need to call in to make that work?*

His dad must have called in the favors, because last year, before Mom found out she was going to have another little sister, his entire family—plus Jax and his parents, another Pack family, and three elves—all flew to California on one of Mr. Freyrsson's charter jets.

Gabe was pretty sure he wasn't the only kid walking around the park that day being tailed by a magical bodyguard. His, though, had been a huge fun-loving guy with sideburns, a ponytail, and an enviable number of Scandinavian death metal t-shirts. A big guy who literally could channel the power of Thor down onto anyone who dared even look at the Martinez family sideways.

Gabe had turned eleven during the trip. At the time, he'd been half annoyed that he was the oldest kid there and didn't have friends along. But he did have Bjorn Thorsson at his side most of the time as consolation, and that alone had meant an elven level of wholesome partying.

As far as Gabe knew, Bjorn hadn't zapped any bad guys while they played at Disneyland. But then again, the elves—and his parents—weren't likely to tell him if there'd been problems.

That had changed last month.

There'd been an issue with the two vampires who'd lived at the now-closed Ramsey Mansion library. Turned out they weren't the Russian Cold War spies they'd pretended to be.

Everyone knew they weren't Russian Cold War spies. The werewolves, the elves, and the mundanes in town who, like Gabe, knew about magic. Mr. Victorsson, too.

Gabe had Mr. Victorsson's number on his cell phone, because Mr. Victorsson wasn't really a mundane, and Mr. Victorsson could knock the head clear off a vampire if he needed to.

Bjorn had called immediately after Dad hung up and given Gabe instructions. Elves were on the way, as were Alfheim's two male alpha werewolves. No one knew where Mr. Victorsson was, but they'd left messages. Gabe was to keep his mother and sisters away from the kelpie until help arrived.

It might be a kelpie, but Gabe was pretty sure there were vampires involved. Otherwise his papa wouldn't have told him to take everyone into the basement.

Vampires were why he'd only been out of Minnesota once. Vampires were why Bjorn and another elf, Sif the Golden, had started training him in ways to protect himself and his siblings. They were going to start training Sophia too, now that she was almost ten, but there'd been new issues there.

Sophia was an oracle.

"No, I am *not* an oracle, dumbass," his little sister said as she helped their little brother, Mateo, with his toys so he wouldn't cry while they were in the basement room.

Gabe shook his head. Only oracles knew when someone else was thinking that they were an oracle.

She narrowed her eyes and shook her head as if to say *Not now. Time's a-wastin', brother.*

They practiced this with Ella and Mateo all the time, just like the tornado drills at school. They practiced with Mom and Dad, and without. With Bjorn or Sif faking that they were something super scary, and without. Ella mostly thought it was boring in her five-year-old way, but Mateo was three. He mostly found it fun because he had unlimited screen time with the good wifi in the room.

Dad had set up the room at the back of the basement, dug out beyond the house's foundation and hidden behind a row of shelves holding their cross-country ski gear. The room wasn't anything nefarious, or weird, or creepy. The previous owner had grown mushrooms, was all. But now the room was charmed and warded, and full of monster slayer stuff.

Momma closed and locked the door to the basement and waddled down the stairs behind the little kids.

"Your sister isn't an oracle, young man," Momma said. She wore a huge sweater and the black stretchy pants she'd had to buy because she'd gotten rid of her maternity clothes after Mateo. She'd been giving away all the baby stuff, too.

Gabe was pretty sure little soon-to-be Grace was not a planned part of their family.

"She's *something*," he said, meaning Sophia, not the new baby.

She was, too. She remembered things about the Alfheim Pack's run under the Samhain moon which, from what he'd been able to pick up, no one else remembered. And they all knew she remembered things they didn't, which meant that she really was remembering things that happened.

Sophia shrugged. "I know what's *true*," she said.

Which could mean anything, magically. And right now, understanding what they were dealing with magically was probably the most important thing to do.

Sophia threw him more side-eye. She looked like a miniature version of their momma, right down to the same pinched-lip frown when she was annoyed. Same dark hair with slight red highlights. Same dark brown eyes they all had. Same keen sense of the situation.

Which was probably why she'd been chosen to be the oracle and he hadn't.

Sophia leaned close to him. "You *were* chosen, but not for *this*." She nodded to their younger siblings. "We were *all* chosen. That's why there's five of us now."

Momma stopped three steps from the basement floor. "What does that mean, honey?" she asked gently.

Sophia hugged Mateo when he grabbed her waist. "There's been a lot of choosings since you and Papa came here," she said. "I don't know what it means." Then she hit Gabe's arm. "Because I'm not the oracle, dumbass."

She said *the* oracle.

"Who's the—"

Upstairs, something slammed into the side of the house.

Sophia slapped her hand over his mouth. "The truth is not for kelpie ears."

That murderous death horse would rip apart his mother and sisters if he got near them.

A mournful wail echoed through the halls upstairs and what first sounded like stallion clomps turned to the steps of a man in boots.

Mom's eyes widened. Her lips rounded, and she looked back at the door.

Ella and Sophia, too, but Sophia stiffened and the tops of her ears turned red.

She grabbed Momma's hand. "He's a *murderer*, Momma."

Momma looked down at her daughter, then at her oldest son. "He's a murderer," she repeated.

"Yes, Momma," Gabe said slowly. "There's a kelpie upstairs. Papa and Bjorn want me to get you, Sophia, and Ella into the room, and for me to hold the key."

Momma looked up the stairs again.

"He's a Scottish fae, Momma," Sophia said. "He lives in a big, deep lake there."

"A loch," Momma said. She didn't move from her spot three steps up the stairs.

"Sophia," Gabe said. "Take Ella and Mateo into the room."

Sophia looked back at him. "The kelpie wants to be our pony," she said.

What was it with little girls and horses? "He's not one of Mr. Freyrsson's horses," Gabe said.

Sophie blinked. Her brow furrowed. "The horses," she mumbled.

"Sophia!" Gabe snapped. "Take Ella and Mateo and *go into the room*."

She looked from him to Momma, and back at him. "We must all go together."

She wasn't an oracle. She didn't know. But he knew deep in his bones that she *knew*.

He nodded. "Momma." He extended his hand. "Your son demands you heed his words."

Bjorn had told him to say that. He'd said, "Channel Old World patriarchy, my smart young friend." Not that Gabe understood what that meant until Bjorn told him to act like every dickhead in every old movie he'd ever seen about long-dead Europeans in puffy clothes.

So he'd act the lordly dickhead if it saved his Momma and sisters.

His mother took two more steps down the stairs. "What did you say to me, young man?"

It was working. "You're going to listen to the man in front of you, understand, woman?"

Sophie chuckled, which caused Ella to chuckle. Mateo just sucked his thumb and looked confused.

Momma looked up the stairs again.

He didn't dare yank on her hand, or try to force her to move. Not so close to her due date. He might accidently knock her off balance or something worse.

He tugged on her hand anyway. "Please, Momma."

She blinked again and looked down at him with her big eyes.

His momma was a beautiful woman. He got to think that because she was his mother, but it was true. She had the round face and strong nose of their Yoreme ancestry, and the height and angles of the Anglo mixed in over the generations. Plus his papa pretty much melted when she walked into the room, and had for as long as Gabe remembered.

The handle on the basement door rattled. "Aye, me loves, a lock's nae enough t' keep me from ye," a melodic male voice said.

The kelpie sounded like one of those guys who did podcasts on the Internet—the ones with the hypnotic voices who sound authoritative, but if you actually thought about the things they said, you knew they were just fast-talking liars using sonic camouflage.

"Momma?"

She inhaled as if an honest-to-goodness movie star had just asked her to marry him.

Sophia held Ella back. "Get between Momma and the door. Now, Gabe!"

The kelpie knocked nicely. "I smell th' lot of ye down there," he said. "The lads, *hmm...*" He paused. "Too bad ye dinnae have a like mind." He paused again. "But ye lassies..." Another pause.

Gabe grabbed the railings and did his best to block his mother from going back up the steps. "Go to the room, Momma," he pleaded.

"I smell a Cassandra down there."

"I am *not* an *oracle!*" Sophia screamed. Her face was totally red now, like she was trying to fight whatever the kelpie was doing to them.

"No' my problem, luv."

A sword blade pierced the door. A big, sharp, scary sword.

Momma screamed. Sophia screamed some more. Ella whimpered and Mateo wailed.

"Ye've nae idea what I had t' do t' get here before th' other elder elves showed up." The sword sliced toward the doorknob. "How fast I had t' gallop t' get away from my love who wants t' feed me t' her cats."

"Momma!" Gabe yelled. "Go!"

She shook like she'd just woken up from a bad dream. "Sophia! Ella! Go!" She swooped down to pick up Mateo but the kelpie…

Gabe had seen magicals do stuff like what the kelpie had just done. Bjorn and Sif had shown him such slight-of-hand tricks as a vampire might use. Or a dark fae.

So he understood about freezing perception in one moment to make a mundane think the magical had moved at lightning speed.

The kelpie was on the other side of him, fully in the basement and standing between his momma and his sisters and brother. He was the same height as Momma, square too, like a tiny linebacker. Black hair, black polo shirt with a hole in it, black kilt, black boots. He looked more like a hooligan than any fae creature.

He held the sword up and away from the kids like he wanted to make sure they didn't get too close. His other arm he used to swoop in and grab Momma around the waist. He moved like he knew how to hold a very pregnant woman, twisting and stepping so as to keep the sword away.

He dipped Gabe's mother in an embrace like some romance novel cover model. "Aye," he said. "My friend th' sheriff understands quality."

He kissed Momma on the lips.

"You are not worthy of finding what you seek," said Sophia. She wasn't screaming anymore. No. She was stone-cold serious.

The kelpie let go of Momma. She gagged and stumbled, but Gabe caught her before she fell.

It had been a reflex move. His focus flitted from his little sister to his falling mother and he responded. He caught his momma before she got hurt.

When he looked up, the kelpie held Sophia at the top of the stairs.

He saluted with the sword.

"Gabe!" His mother pushed at him and the wall. "Go! Go with your sister. Please!"

She grimaced and cupped her belly.

He knew what the pain meant. "Momma!"

"The elves are coming. I'll be..." She grimaced again. "We'll be fine. Go!"

So Gabriel Martinez, the soon-to-be thirteen-year-old son of the local sheriff, chased after the kelpie who'd kidnapped his sister.

CHAPTER 18

The kelpie turned off their phones and tossed them into the back of Momma's minivan. Then he tossed Sophia into the backseat. "Sit down, darlin'." He used the sword to point at the driver's door as he pulled the key fob from one of the many tactical pockets on his kilt. "Ye're drivin', boy."

Gabe Martinez stood on the step into the house directly between the kelpie and the door handle—and his Momma. "I don't have a learner's permit," he said. He couldn't get his permit for another two years, but his dad had taken him out to the empty parking lot in front of the City Management Complex and taught him the basics.

They all had to be ready for emergencies, his father had told him. Know your magicals, kiddo. Understand the basic rules for interactions: No exchanges of any kind. No food. No promises. No secrets.

And always squeeze the trigger. Never jerk your hand.

The kelpie sniffed the air like a dog. "Aye, 'tis true." The kelpie touched the side of his nose, then pointed at Gabe. "But ye're th' son of a lawman who lives under a cloud of threatenin' darkness." He tapped his own forehead. "An' ye live in th' middle of frickin' nowhere in th' middle of a middle state in a middlin' country." He sniffed at the air again. "So a guess about you gettin' early drivin' lessons ain't so farfetched, lad."

He shook his momma's key fob again and tapped the driver's door with the tip of the sword.

Gabe snatched the fob from the kelpie's hand.

"Wait until I'm in, kiddo," the kelpie said.

Gabe didn't answer. Getting in and locking the door wouldn't help. The kelpie would just cut the minivan into metal ribbons.

But he could open the garage door.

There *had* to be an elf or two out there by now. Maybe even the Pack. If he opened the garage door—

"Ye let in th' puppies, I'll slice yer wee sister," the kelpie growled.

So the Pack *was* outside.

Gabe slid into the driver's seat of their minivan. Slowly and as calmly as he could manage, he reviewed what his dad had taught him: Accelerator on the right. Brake on the left. R means reverse and D means drive. Press the brake before starting the vehicle. Hands at two and ten on the steering wheel. And look. Always look, even with the cameras all over the van. At least his momma and papa always backed the vehicles into the garage, so he wouldn't have to deal with turning the van around.

The kelpie dropped into the front passenger seat and placed his big sword between his hairy legs. He looked around the inside, opening and closing the van's many cubbies, until he opened the center console and found Momma's stash of little kid snacks.

"Ah!" He slapped his thigh. "Apple! My favorite." He snapped a straw into a juice box and took a long, slurping draw.

"I'm cold," Sophia said from the backseat.

The kelpie didn't seem cold in his holey black polo shirt and kilt. The douchebag scruff on his chin was probably keeping him toasty warm. "Ah, darlin', I do apologize. We'll be on our way shortly an' yer dear brother here will start up this beastie's heatin' system, aye?"

Gabe gripped the steering wheel. "Why don't you just gallop away?"

114

He shouldn't have asked the question. Don't interact with dark fae. Don't give them *any* room to stick in a knife and force you to make a deal.

But maybe he could logic his way out of this situation. His teachers did like to tell him he was good at figuring out how to fix a moment. Ms. Sagasdottir wanted him to "cultivate his leadership ability." That's why he'd joined 4-H even though at first he hadn't wanted to.

"I didnae gallop away," the kelpie said, "because this toothpick here," he tapped the pommel on the sword, "ain't trade-worthy, wi' th' teeths."

He bared his teeth and made a little fangy-face as he sipped at his apple juice.

"We are," Sophia said. "Us, and Papa."

The kelpie nodded. "Cassandra has spoken."

No asking questions. Don't give the kelpie an opening.

So Gabe asked his sister, instead. "Do you know why, Sophia?"

The kelpie slurped and looked around the headrest. "Do tell, luv."

"You are not worthy." She said no more.

The kelpie shrugged. "Clearly." He crumpled the empty box and tossed it into the back of the van. "There are two alpha werewolves outside." He sniffed the air. "An' three elves out there." He sniffed again. "Two Thor an' a Frigg," he frowned. "Where's that utterly *perfect* female who wants this?" He patted the pommel again. "Ah, my soul's hers."

Utterly perfect applied equally to all the elves, so Gabe didn't know if he meant Queen Dagrun, or Akeyla's mom, or Benta the Nameless, or one of his teachers.

"Ms. Benta won't let Jax visit the cats," Sophia said.

The kelpie laughed. "Lovely *an'* mean. My kind o' lass." He inhaled. "Th' big Thor elf is... angry."

Bjorn was out there. He was the biggest elf in Alfheim. Not magic-wise—that was the King and the Queen, and probably Mr. Magnus, too—but size-wise. He wasn't obviously taller than any of the other elves—they were all tall like Vikings were supposed to be—but he was significantly wider, with wide elf sideburns and an extra-thick elf ponytail, even if he still somehow managed to hold most of his glamour and keep his pointy ears disguised as round and normal.

Bjorn Thorsson was equal parts the bear of his first name and the Thor of his last.

"Mr. Bjorn is older than the United States," Sophia said from the back seat.

The kelpie shrugged. "As am I, m' wee lass."

"Mr. Bjorn is older than *Scotland*," Sophia said.

The kelpie shrugged again.

She leaned forward, between the seats. "Mr. Bjorn hasn't killed you yet because he wants to make sure Mr. Lennart and Ms. Sif get Momma and the little kids out safely."

"They need nae worry." The kelpie pulled out another apple juice box. "Ye two know it's *ye* I want."

"Mr. Bjorn knows, too. So does Mr. Magnus. He's had his fill of fae for the day. And Ms. Benta is *mean*."

"I want ye 'cause ye're an oracle, darlin'."

"And you are a moron," Sophia responded.

"Sophia…" Gabe whispered.

She continued to stare at the kelpie. "It's okay," she said. "He knows I'm not lying."

The kelpie frowned as he slurped at his new juice box until it also collapsed into a shriveled ball of carton. He looked at it as if it had forsaken not only him, but all his ancestors as well. Then he tossed it into the back of the van, too.

"Yer definition o' *moron* differs from mine, sweetling," the kelpie said. "I blame linguistic drift." He wagged a finger at her. "Kids these days."

"We understand what you are," Gabe said.

The kelpie nodded. "Ah, ye do, don't ye? So I guess we cannae be friends, then, aye?"

"Gabe wishes to use several swear words to describe you right now," Sophia said.

He did.

"Oh, my lad. See, ye an' I, we could be great friends. I could teach ye all th' Scottish swears yer little-man heart desires an' I guarantee ye th' parental types will find it so charmin' no one grounds ye." He winked.

"No exchanges with a dark fae," Gabe said.

The kelpie sniffed. His eyes narrowed. "Th' sad truth here is tha' I'm nae match for th' elves out there."

"They know that," Sophia said.

"That Benta one could literally pop my head like I'm some kind o' fae zit but she's concerned about what seein' that will do to their monster slayer's offspring."

"Yes," Sophia said.

"But mostly she's worried about how th' sword will react," the kelpie whispered.

The sword was covered with runes that didn't look right, and was too gray and dull to be truly one of the elves' weapons, but the kelpie sure thought it was.

"Which is why it's here wi' us," the kelpie finished.

Sophia dropped her gaze to the sword. She stared silently at it for a long moment, then she sat back without saying a word.

"Yer silence says more than anythin' else, oracle," the kelpie said.

"Not an oracle," Sophia responded.

The kelpie sniffed again. "Th' other Thor elf is carryin' yer ma out the back door, my young friends." He sniffed again. "That other elf, the female who glamours up all blonde an' bohemian is carin' fer yer wee siblings." Another sniff. "Strong magicks, there."

Of course they're strong magicks, Gabe thought.

The kelpie slapped the dash. "All right, my wee friends!" He inhaled deeply. "It's time."

Gabe wouldn't plead. Pleading would lead to a deal, and a deal would be worse than getting hurt, so he just waited for the kelpie to give him instructions.

The kelpie tapped his fingers along the pommel, then he did something that said he had magic in his hand: He flipped his fingers the way a magician flips a quarter between his knuckles.

Gabe had no idea what spellwork he pinched between his thumb and forefinger like a coin, but he had something there. Something that he brushed against the sword's blade.

"*Hmmm….*" The kelpie pointed at the garage door without looking at Gabe. "Turn on th' van, son," he said.

Should he?

"He won't let us open the garage door unless you turn on the van," Sophia said.

His not-an-oracle sister wanted him to open the door.

Gabe pressed his foot into the brake and his finger into the starter.

Then he hit the garage door opener.

The kelpie slammed the sword into the floorboards so it stood up on its own. "Drive!" he barked.

The garage door rose enough so the pavement of the driveway came into view. A little bit of snow. Some ice. No people.

Gabe put his hand on the gear shift. He was pretty sure he had to press, push, and wiggle to get it to move. He looked back at the slowly revealing driveway.

Where was everyone? Why wasn't his father right there, gun out, and yelling for the kelpie to get out of the van?

The door continued to rise. He looked back at the gear shift. If he purposefully messed up putting the van in drive, would the kelpie hurt them?

He looked back at the driveway. And there, at the end, parked in such a way as to make it impossible to get the van out or around and onto the street, sat two Alfheim County Sheriff's Department vehicles.

One was the fake K-9 Unit meant for the Pack. The other was his father's cruiser.

His papa was here. He'd made it back from wherever he was, out on the roads, all the way to Alfheim in the time Gabe and Sophia had been stalling the kelpie.

"Papa's here," he breathed, before he realized he should have kept that info to himself.

But his father had come to save them. Gabe looked back at his sister.

She clamped her hand onto his arm and stared wide-eyed at the cars outside. "Duck!" Sophia screamed.

Gabe looked back at the vehicles just as two werewolves leaped at the van.

CHAPTER 19

E d Martinez would take his wife and children far, far from Alfheim and the Gulf Coast. He'd take them into Ontario, or the interior of Oregon, or deep into Mexico, if he had to.

All these damned magicals were way too dangerous.

The fae lawwoman pointed. "The elves have your wife and the younger children. They're taking them through the backyard to the next street over."

Lennart Thorsson and Sif the Golden were moving his pregnant wife and two youngest through the neighbor's yard. They'd get them into Lennart's SUV and immediately take them to Alfheim's hospital where they would be checked over and placed under the direct protection of Alfheim's Elf Queen, Dagrun Tyrsdottir.

And Wrenn saw it all because she saw magic.

He wasn't going to think about her connections to Alfheim's tall, maroon-eyed, magic-seeing local right now. The elves could deal with that.

Bjorn Thorsson seemed much more interested in the sword the damned kelpie had stolen off Wrenn than he was in Wrenn herself, even with the magic-seeing. So it was probably a good thing no one could find Frank Victorsson.

The big elf wasn't glamouring well at the moment. Ed's neighbors, many of whom were likely watching from their windows, would see the owner of Raven's Gaze outside the Sheriff's house, which was weird enough. The visible blue electrical static dancing on his shoulders might cause a panic.

The elves could deal with that, too.

Bjorn moved his hands as if whipping up a spell.

Wrenn watched Bjorn's hands, then peered at Ed's garage door. "I'm not seeing any spikes in Ranger's magicks," she said.

Bjorn nodded. "Do *not* engage *any* of your fae spells." He didn't look at her. "Do *not* interfere with my or any of the others' enchantments. We cannot have you accidently waking up the sword again." Magnus Freyrsson and Benta the Nameless were nearby but hidden. Ed didn't know where. Neither did Wrenn, and Bjorn wasn't going to say.

Wrenn nodded.

"Follow the Sheriff's lead. Stay with him and to the side of the driveway until we have a clear path to the children," Bjorn continued.

The magicals would contain the kelpie and the sword while Ed went in for the kids. The concealment enchantments woven from the vehicles to the house should keep Ed and Wrenn invisible until they reached the van.

Wrenn nodded again.

"And stay away from Redemption. We will deal with her."

Ed had guessed the sword's full name the moment Wrenn told him it had called itself Red. It fit the pattern. "That sword talked to her, Bjorn," he said.

Bjorn did not flinch, or respond in any way, which meant that somewhere in that elven head he was thinking what they were all thinking: Wrenn was a piece on a game board here, and someone better figure out the rules.

He'd leave that to the elves, too.

Wrenn raised her hands. "Red's your problem, not mine."

They were reacting as if Ranger held the nuclear football. Which he might. The sword was why Magnus Freyrsson and Benta the Nameless were out there, somewhere, waiting.

A little voice in the back of Ed's head said that they weren't the only elves surrounding his house. All of the elder elves were probably here, including Arne Odinsson and his daughter, Maura Dagsdottir.

He really did have to get his family out of here.

Bjorn moved his hands again. His spells weren't for Ranger. They were meant to conceal the two magicals sitting directly in front of the garage door.

Gerard and Remy Geroux, both in their dire wolf form, sat in Ed's driveway about ten feet from the door. Neither wore vests, but if there were questions, the fake K-9 unit behind which Ed stood would provide cover.

Even if the kelpie smelled the wolves coming, the spells meant he wouldn't see them.

"We will increase protections on your family," Bjorn rumbled. "The whole city." He sniffed as he flipped his hands. "The *state*." His lip twitched and the blue dancing along his shoulders brightened. "This will *never* happen to your children again, Eduardo Martinez. On this, I swear."

Wrenn's lips rounded for a split second as if this was the first time in her life she'd seen a magical vow to protect mundanes.

It wasn't Ed's. Usually they did a good enough job.

Usually.

Ed looked up at the huge elf. Bjorn's jaw worked. He was barely containing his rage.

"If that kelpie harms any of our mundanes, I will lay waste to Oberon's realm," Bjorn rumbled. He didn't look at Wrenn.

She blinked again. "Noted," she said.

This was not a normal elven display. Not even close. And frankly, even though Bjorn was here to protect Ed's family, his reaction was epic-battle-ready level behavior. The elf looked moments from manifesting his elven armor.

Wrenn continued to watch Bjorn with wide eyes as if she figured he'd burst open at any moment. Which he might.

"The van's engine just engaged," Bjorn raised his hands. "Go!"

The werewolves literally vanished behind concealment enchantments. Bjorn, too.

Wrenn blinked. "I can't see their magicks."

Ed slapped the SUV and motioned for her to move with him, slow and steady, along the side of the driveway toward the door. "The enchantments are working."

She stepped in front of him. "I can take any blasts from Ranger. Stay behind me."

Except she couldn't. He'd overpowered her in the park. But she seemed to believe that to be a fluke.

Ed nodded anyway and stayed slightly behind her, but not so much so he couldn't fire his shotgun if he needed to.

They were halfway up the driveway when the garage door lifted enough to give the werewolves a clear line of vision.

"Duck!" Sophia screamed from inside.

Gerard Geroux manifested as he leaped onto the hood of their family van.

He'd changed behind the concealments.

In their human forms, Gerard and Remy were two of Alfheim's most upstanding citizens. Both were Scout troop leaders. Gerard would plow out your driveway if he happened to be in the area. They donated a lot of time and money to just about every good cause in the county.

What hit the van scared the crap out of Ed.

Ten years in Alfheim and Ed had only seen a werewolf in wolfman form twice, and neither of them had been one of the alphas.

They hadn't told him they were going do this. They'd only said the Alphas would go in first and distract Ranger.

Gerard still had the tail and the wolf head, and the bulk of his brown-black fur, but he was definitely human. A human with big wolf teeth, and huge wolf claws.

Ed's son sat in the driver's seat, eyes wide and white with terror. Sophia, in the back, gaped at the werewolf. That slimeball Ranger had the damned sword between his legs and it stood straight up like he'd jabbed the tip into the floor of the van.

Ed and Wrenn were five feet from the open garage door when Gerard locked his claws into the windshield.

Sophia didn't open the side door to escape. She leaned forward and clasped her brother's bicep, putting herself directly in the werewolf's path.

Something was wrong.

The glass shrieked and buckled, lifting up away from the van under Gerard's claws like it was paper, and pulled away from its seal to the automobile.

The windshield popped out and folded over in Gerard's hand like a twinkling glass cape.

The kids ducked and screamed. Ranger looked directly at Wrenn. He grinned.

She looked down at her wrist.

Gerard tossed the glass into the driveway.

"Stop!" Wrenn yelled. "He took my Heartway token!"

Ranger slapped one of his hands over Sophia's hand on Gabe's bicep.

"Red! *Don't!*" Wrenn leaped toward the van and grabbed the driver's side door handle.

But Remy was there, leaping from God knows where, also in wolfman form, diving to bite Ranger's arm right off and to get between the kelpie and Ed's kids.

Ranger slapped his other hand, the one with his little coin of magic, onto the hilt of the sword.

The damned sword went nuclear.

And Ed's garage vanished.

CHAPTER 20

The sword screamed. Searing pain blasted from her, hot like the sun, bound and burning and bidden from Muspelheim. Ranger had somehow woken her up.

Except she wasn't awake. He'd pulled her nightmares to the surface and they were all about to pay the price of whatever spells the fae had used to bind a powerful elven weapon.

Each Heartway token was an access key. It allowed passage into what was essentially a system of spellwork tunnels built within the many veils between the many realms. And the veil between the fae realms and the real world.

Wrenn didn't have the power needed to open gates. Neither did Ranger. But Ranger was fae, and Ranger was magical.

Wrenn looked down at her wrist. Ranger was also a thief.

And, it seemed, he was better at being all those things than anyone thought possible.

Wrenn looked back at the van as the wolfman tossed the glass into the driveway. The second one leaped. They were almost between Ranger and the kids. But it didn't matter.

"Stop!" Wrenn yelled. "He took my Heartway token!" Not that the elves or the other members of their community would understand what she meant.

Ranger, in the passenger seat of Sheriff Martinez's van, clamped a hand down on top of the girl's hand on her brother's arm.

We bind thee, Fenrir! the sword shrieked. *We bind thee near!*

Red wasn't in this moment. She was dreaming and blasting off wave after wave of magical power.

Power a better-than-average kelpie could channel into an access spell.

"Red!" Maybe Wrenn could wake her up. *"Don't!"* She leaped toward the van and grabbed the driver's side door handle.

Ranger slapped Wrenn's Heartway token onto Redemption's hilt.

We bind thee—

Ranger closed his eyes and pushed his head into the headrest. The boy looked up at Wrenn, his big brown eyes wide and determined. And the girl...

The girl knew what was happening. She inhaled deeply at the same time she slapped her free hand over Ranger's mouth and nose.

"We'll find—" Wrenn started to say. She'd gotten her hand around the door handle. The wolfmen were inches from getting between Ranger and the kids but that girl *knew.*

And she did what she needed to do to protect her brother.

What had to be Redemption's nightmare burst outward from her hilt like an infinitely fast bubble. Ranger vanished into it first. The kids second. Then it came for the wolfmen.

The one on the hood twisted just as Ranger slapped the token onto Red's hilt. His shoulder came around and he scooped his arm around his brother's chest but they were closer than Wrenn. And they were magicals in the way of a magic explosion.

The bubble hit Wrenn.

She still had her hand on the van's door handle. The kids still sat in the seats. Red still stood stuck into the floor between Ranger's feet. But the world around them changed.

She'd been in Heartway stations many times. They tended to manifest like mass transit rail stations—gates and platforms and waiting benches. Whistling trains for effect and big ticking clocks to remind everyone to move along. Crumpled newspapers on the ground. The scent of oranges or flowers or snow in the air.

But she'd never stood on the rails.

There was no station here. No gateway. Just the lines.

And this place of elves had *lines.*

"Ley lines" was what the fae called them. The elves didn't seem to care or utilize the power lines of the Earth, so she doubted they understood what King Oberon was doing underneath the veils. Or maybe they did.

Because here, inside this particular veil, something here in Alfheim out on the edge of town glowed like the busiest station in all the worlds.

She looked back at Ranger, the kids, the sword, and the van door she still gripped.

Ranger opened his eyes. His chin pointed toward the wolfmen.

Except he wasn't pointing at the wolfmen. He was pointing at the Heartway car, or train, or bubble of spellwork, or enchantment—the name or metaphor didn't matter—that was about to hit the bubble of power emanating from Redemption.

And then they were gone. All of it—Ranger, the kids, the sword, the damned van and the floor of the garage and the side of the house. All gone, taken by the Heartway to...

Wrenn gasped. Her head spun and her ears rang and she dropped into the new pit that used to be the lawman's garage. She fell and stumbled, and did her best to stay out of the way of the two also-falling werewolves.

The magic had burned both of them, singed off their fur on the side closest to Redemption. No singes on her, no burns or cuts, either. Just the ringing ears. The wolf who had been in the air when Ranger slapped the token onto the sword—the one named Remy, if she remembered correctly—howled in pain.

The hot tang of werewolf blood hit her nose. Remy's arm was broken and he bled from a gash across his chest.

The other one snapped at her as she stumbled down the slick side of the pit.

"The wolves are hurt! We need elves down here *now!*" She held up her hands. "I'll get you help."

The big one, Gerard was his name, howled.

Redemption, she thought. *What did you do?*

A gateway into a desert. Heat. Still night, like here. She knew these things, even though no one told her, or showed her, or communicated to her in any conscious way.

She was still connected to the sword. She had to be.

Ed looked over the edge of the pit. "Where are my children?" he bellowed.

She threw out her hands as if surrounded by ghosts. "Red!" She *felt* the sword. How long would her connection to the sword hold? "They're in Texas," she told the wolves. "Ed!" She reached out her hand. "I feel the sword!"

He immediately stuck out his foot to slide into the pit.

The big Thor elf grabbed his arm. "No. Let us handle this."

The elves needed to let Ed handle it. They were his kids. They needed him. "Let him go!" she yelled. She could get him into the Heartway. "Ed, I can follow."

He pulled away from the elf and slid into the pit. "You better not be lying to me."

"If you can carry out your brother, do it now," she said to Gerard.

He sniffed at her with his wolf nose, then looked down at Remy.

Gerard Geroux lifted his wounded brother and bounded up the side of the crater.

How was she going to do this? She didn't have a token, and there weren't stations here.

But there were lines—lines she'd seen when Red exploded.

"As a Paladin of King Oberon, I hereby officially request law enforcement backup from the Sheriff of Alfheim County." She looked the Sheriff directly in the eye. "This is not a deal. This is parallel behavior."

He nodded once.

She looked up at Bjorn Thorsson. "I need you to hit me with whatever magic the sword gave off."

His lip curled.

"I can hear her!" Wrenn yelled. "She's talking to me. I can follow!"

"Then you take *me*," the big elf said.

"I cannot take an elf into the Heartway." Probably. Most likely. She'd never tried. Now was not the time to accidentally kill an elder elf.

She could move a mundane, though.

"We'll call you the moment we have a specific location," Ed yelled.

Wrenn nodded. "They're in Texas," she said.

Bjorn looked over his shoulder. He stiffened. "I'm sending them!" he snapped.

There was another elf up there. Another powerful one.

A sigil formed in front of Bjorn's hands. He twisted his fingers and straightened his arms and all the blue electrical fire that had been dancing along his shoulders moved to his magic.

Wrenn pulled Ed close. "Hold on," she said, just as an elf named Bjorn hit her full force with the electrical power of the sky.

CHAPTER 21

The elves had run Ed's family through a gauntlet of magical approximations the moment they'd set foot in Alfheim, so he knew what it meant to be inside magic. "Expect spells to feel this way" with fae, and "that way" with kami, they said. These spirits will feel slighted "if you do this" and those spirits "if you do that." Mostly, don't bother the magic and it won't bother you.

Hold still and let it spin out. Concentrate on how it's changing the world around you. Respond to the changes, not the magic itself.

Except it never worked that way in Alfheim. Or Texas. Or anywhere. Mostly because the magic wasn't going to leave you alone long enough for you to get your bearings.

Bjorn called down the power of Thor to do whatever it was Wrenn had asked. He hit them with energy so strong it changed the cold, clean scent of winter air to the acrid ozone smell of a terrifying electrical storm. But this place called the Heartway? It burned like they'd actually been hit by a real bolt of lightning.

No, like Ed stood inside of a bolt of lightning.

"You need to stay in physical contact with me until we catch a gate," Wrenn said.

There was still breathable atmosphere here, even with the ozone and the flat white—or colorless—nothingness around them. He heard her words and wasn't gasping for air. "Okay."

There was nothing here. Nothing he perceived, at least. "You said this place is like a railway," he said. As far as he could tell, the Heartway was empty, though up and down still counted, and left and right. No rail lines or trains—though he had a strong sense that there were lines here.

"It is," she said. "Except we're not in a station."

He lowered his shotgun and stepped in front of her. She was taller. She could see around him, and it would be better overall if they both saw whatever was coming at the same time.

"I'm not seeing anything other than..." How was he supposed to describe it? "There's ground here. I'm pretty sure I see ground. But I'm not really registering the ground. Does that make sense?"

"Rail lines need to travel through territory," she said. "This place is the equivalent to magical open country. A no-man's-land of sorts. It's between realms. Inside the veils."

"Are we between The Land of the Living and The Land of the Dead?" Because Frank had talked about moving between The Lands of the Living and the Dead.

Ed being dead would not help anyone.

"No," Wrenn said. "The places inside the veils are... primordial, I guess. That's why there's nothing here. Nothing's been built."

Behind him, Wrenn reached into her jacket to pull out her phone. "I need to figure out where we are in the system." A few swipes and she held out the phone as if looking for a connection. "Come on."

She expected service. Inside a primordial magical place.

Reflexively, Ed pulled out his own phone.

No bars on his. "Yours works?"

Hers trilled. "The fae have been teching-up these past fifteen years or so."

"What carrier is working with magicals?" This was all too weird.

"It's the King's system. The Queen calls it TwinkleBell." She twisted it around. "There." Several apps unfolded like little dancing pixies landing on her screen. One in particular lit up. "We aren't anywhere near a stop but the map says there are trains nearby. The problem is Texas is a big place."

"But you can still hear the sword, correct?"

She tilted her head. "Not in here." Her lip twitched.

So they were blind. Unless...

Ed held out his phone. "I can see the kids' phones." Unless that kelpie turned them off. "The van's got a GPS tracer on it." But his phone didn't have service.

"*Heh*," she said, and touched her phone to his.

Every single app on his phone transferred to hers, and probably his passwords, too. "You better not tell the elves fae magic can do that."

"I'll wipe it off my phone when this is over." She tapped at his tracker app.

"You do that," he said. "The moment we get back to Alfheim." With his kids. Because they'd be returning with the kids or they wouldn't be returning at all.

Wrenn tucked away her phone. "Put that away and prepare yourself," she said.

Ed tucked his phone back into his pocket and readied his shotgun.

"Step with me." Wrenn moved him about six strides to the left. "This is going to hurt." She wrapped an arm around his shoulders. "Don't hold your—"

Something hit him square in the chest. And gut. And head. He fell and—

He landed on his back and his head bounced off a rough wooden floor. His lungs sucked in heavy, wet, electricity-filled air. Raindrops hit his face even though he was inside, blinking through the blue-white glare of this place.

He wasn't moving. The jars lining the walls rattled but not from travel on any train tracks. They rattled because of the electrical power roaring off the tall metal rod sticking through the roof.

Frank came to the elves because the power of Thor brought him back to life, he thought. But he was pretty sure it wasn't that simple, and that he shouldn't care anyway, and that he had a task in this moment that had nothing to do with Frank Victorsson.

Ed was here for his kids.

He flexed to sit but a huge hand, fingers steepled and spread out, touched his chest as if to cage his heart.

A face appeared from the glare. "Well, well, what do we have here?"

A bolt scar on the side of his face. Deep maroon, fire-filled eyes. Fangs.

Frank's brother stared down at Ed as if he was a beer and a bag of chips.

Ed swung the shotgun around, but the monster grabbed the barrel.

"Never shoot the conductor," the monster said. He looked up at the huge lightning rod. "The Heartway takes what it wants to get you where you need to be."

"How are you taking from me what it needs?" Ed asked.

The monster looked down at him again. "You?" He sniffed at the air in much the same way as that damned kelpie. "Ah, yes. There *is* something tasty there. It hurt, didn't it? Killing that vampire?"

There was no point in lying. No point in puffing himself up or giving this fae manifestation even a hint that he wasn't at peace with what he did. "Nothing hurt worse," he said.

Never in his life had Ed been so personal with violence. Never in his few years as a deputy, even with the violent types in Santo Guijarro county. He'd seen blood, yes. Gunshot wounds, and severed limbs in that one car crash. But nothing like what had happened in that dim, moldy room in real Texas, which hadn't been much different than the one conjured by the Heartway for Wrenn Goodfellow.

There'd also been glass jars there, in Texas. And body parts.

The monster—the conductor—sniffed. "*Ah…*"

And this place shifted.

There'd been an autopsy table, too, but unlike the Heartway room's table, the vamp's had been on the floor. Ed inhaled sharply. The strangers from Minnesota who said they were magical—they *were* magical, he'd seen one turn into a frickin' wolf—were supposed to be here. They were supposed to help.

He had a baby boy at home. He was a deputy. He wasn't supposed to deal with serial killers.

He hit that vampire with the butt of his shotgun. The vile thing winced enough to allow Ed sufficient leverage to roll away. He shot out a window. Light streamed in. The vamp screamed.

Ed curb-stomped the monster's head against the edge of the autopsy table.

The shift reversed.

The monster—not the vamp in Texas, the conductor—sniffed at his face. "Slayer," he whispered. He sniffed again then sat up. "I will give you a boon, little mundane: You are right to fear what you fear."

What the hell did that mean? Damned fae and their tricks.

The monster pointed at Ed's face and laughed. "I like you!" He lifted his other hand off Ed's chest and nodded over his shoulder. "You're not the one who's supposed to have the token, little mundane."

Ed lifted his head to look.

Wrenn stood in the threshold of a door. Darkness roiled behind her as if there wasn't a room back there, only void. She wore a loose white shift of a dress, one with a tie at the neck that stretched open enough he saw her shoulder. Her hair hung free and cascaded down her back like black fire.

Neither the shift nor her hair covered her scars. One coiled up the from her chest and around another, smaller, star-shaped scar. Then it ran up the side of her neck where it sprouted into a tree-like pattern on the side of her face. Yet another, darker scar ran down her right arm.

A man stepped between her and the monster. His clothes were some sort of old style, the kind with floppy shirts and pants that only buttoned. His short hair was messy like he'd just gotten out of the shower, or moved out from under the rain leaking in from the ceiling. His eyes gleamed the same blue as the electricity surrounding the rod.

That's Victor Frankenstein, Ed thought.

Victor snatched Wrenn's arm and yanked her toward him, all while staring wide-eyed and terrified at the monster. She didn't respond, or pull away, even when he licked her cheek. She just watched her vampire brother.

The monster bolted off Ed and straight for the man.

The Wrenn Ed knew manifested between him and where the monster grabbed hold of Victor Frankenstein. The modern Wrenn without scars, whose soul had been bared to him by this place. The one wearing the black leather jacket. She grabbed him by the shoulders and lifted his upper body off the floor.

Behind her, a snap. Then a wet ripping. A gurgle.

Wrenn squeezed her eyes shut. "I'm sorry you had to see that."

She slammed him against the hard, dry, dusty Texas ground.

CHAPTER 22

P ebbles bounced along the dry ground away from Ed and
Wrenn's shuffling feet.

She gasped and rolled away from him, her hand over the left side
of her face as if he'd just slashed her cheek.

He hadn't. Someone—*something*—had, right where Victor had
licked the aspect of Wrenn in the white dress. Blood seeped through
her fingers.

"You okay?" The elves never did anything like that. Not that kind
of blood magic.

Wrenn gasped again and... flickered.

Ed blinked. Was it the shadows? His eyes hadn't adjusted to the
gloom. Except he'd seen flickers like that before, when a glamour
broke.

"I didn't have a token." She looked at the blood on her hand. "The
Heartway took... other things."

Something in his mind flickered as if an internal glamour wavered.
Not now, he thought. He hadn't had a flashback to his boot coming
down on that vamp's jaw in years. To how much different vampire
blood smelled from mundane blood. To...

He rubbed his face. Damned fae magic took a slice out of his brain.

"Did you..." He shook and tapped his own temple.

Her eyes narrowed. "It *can't* take from you. You're a mundane."

So are you, he thought.

She patted at the cut on her cheek. It, at least, had already stopped bleeding.

The Heartway had showed Ed something he shouldn't have seen. Not only his own flashback, but hers, too. He nodded once and let it be. It wasn't his place to add to the invasion.

Wrenn staggered to her feet and moved into the shadows. She obviously needed a moment.

He looked around. Crumbling adobe walls surrounded where they landed. To their west, a gap in the wall showed the final salmons and pinks of evening as they spread over the horizon. To their east, another gap in the walls—pretty much only the corners of the building still stood—revealed thick brush. Something skittered away, probably a horned lizard, and vanished under a jumble of branches. Birds chirped. Somewhere in the distance, a coyote yipped.

Ed inhaled. A heavy Gulf of Mexico breeze slapped humidity against his nose and sinuses.

They'd landed inside the remains of an old mission somewhere on the Gulf Coast, not far from the ocean.

Wrenn wiped the blood onto her black pants. "This building used to be the local equivalent to Manny's Backwoods Lodge in the Paul Bunyan Forest. Such places tend to harbor unused Heartway stops."

She waved as if she refused to say any more.

So no more talk of the Heartway and its heart-ripping ways, which was fine with him.

She extended her hand to help him up. "We should be in a place called Laguna Atascosa National Wildlife Refuge."

Overhead, stars shimmered in the evening sky—and a dull glow danced along the horizon to the south.

They were near a town. A big one, too, from the light pollution.

The town was likely Brownsville, which meant they weren't anywhere near Santo Guijarro County. But it also meant they were considerably closer to South Padre Island—and one of the most powerful Gulf Coast vampire clans.

American vampires were not Old World vampires. American vampires were new money, relatively speaking. American vampires were corporate.

Lots of shipping money, in New Orleans. Lots of oil money, in Texas. And all along the coast from the Everglades to South Padre, lots of tourist destinations, especially destinations where transient young people liked to get drunk and act stupid.

American vampires were as American as baseball, apple pie, and tax evasion.

Ed dusted off his knees and tied his jacket around his waist. Winter temperatures in South Texas were normal summer temperatures in Minnesota, and he'd overheat damned fast if he didn't drop the coat. "Is he taking them to the Claytons?" he asked as he stripped off his hat and stuck it into his back pocket.

Wrenn frowned. She didn't seem fazed by the change in temperature, which shouldn't come as a surprise. He'd seen her brother—not her vampire brother, but Frank Victorsson—walk around totally unfazed by temperature changes, too.

And after the little bit of privacy invasion he'd just witnessed in the Heartway, he was one hundred percent certain that Alfheim's elf-raised son of Victor had a fae-raised sister.

All of which he stuffed into his Wrenn Goodfellow file in the back of his mind.

"Warren Clayton Jr., patriarch of Clayton Gas and Oil, master of his domain, and owner of half of South Padre Island via an intricate web of shell corporations." Wrenn pulled out her phone again. "Warren Clayton, Jr. also happens to be the one and only Warren Clayton of Belfast, a grifter of a man born right around the same time as I was." She held the device again as if looking for service. "And one of the first Anglos in this area." She tapped at the screen. "His son disappeared about ten years ago."

She knew more about the clans than he did. "You and I are going to share notes when this is done," he said.

Wrenn looked him up and down. "No deals, remember, Sheriff? Not even with fae-adjacent witches."

There was that witch thing again. He filed that, too. "Where are my kids?"

Unlike Paul Bunyan, reserves in this part of Texas were full of roads and trails. If Ranger got the van onto a flatter surface, he'd have them out and to the vamps in no time.

He pulled out his phone and called up the GPS tracker.

According to the app, the van was literally on top of them.

He cocked his head, listening for little clicks, or small noises, or dust settling. And there, just on the other side of the south wall, a small *tick* of a cooling engine.

"Gabe!" he shouted. "Sophia!" He bolted around the adobe.

The van teetered on a pile of what was left of his garage. The door into the house stuck out from under the back tires, and the garage door under the front. The concrete of the floor lay strewn about like beach sand. His snowblower sat on its side against the adobe of the old mission.

No way the van, even if it had been capable of moving, would have gotten off that rubble in one piece.

"Where are my kids?" He peered into the bush. "Gabe! Sophia!" he called again as he scrambled up the rubble pile.

The van was empty. He peered in through the back windows looking for any clue. "The kids' phones."

"Careful!" Wrenn called from down below.

Ed crawled in through the open back passenger door. No blood. No burn marks, either, which was good. He fished the phones out of the back and tucked them into his pockets with his own. "I don't think they're wounded."

Wrenn closed her eyes as if listening. "He can move fast in stallion form," she said.

Ed clambered down the rubble pile. "How fast? Which direction? Are they riding him? Riding a kelpie is seriously bad juju, isn't it?"

Was one of his kids carrying that damned sword like it was Excalibur or something? He had a flash of Gabe dealing with all the crap that came with being the Once and Future King.

Because they needed *that*, too.

"Ranger won't hurt them," said Wrenn. Her expression said the rest of what she was thinking: He'll leave that for the vampires.

That kelpie wasn't going to survive this. He'd be dead before the sun came up. Either the vamps would kill him, or the elves would.

Or Ed would do it himself.

Ranger had crossed the line from capture-and-detain to clear-and-present-danger the moment he'd stepped out of the fae realms. He, like the vamps, was the magical equivalent of a rabid animal.

Ed pulled out his own phone and dialed. "Bjorn," he said. "We're in Laguna Atascosa National Wildlife Refuge near South Padre Island." He hung up. The elves might be able to dial themselves in with their magic in some sort of Heartway way... but he'd never seen them do so. Ever. They flew in airplanes like everyone else.

Which meant they'd be here in the morning, at the earliest.

Wrenn peered through the trees. "The clans want you, not your kids, Ed."

Ed wasn't so sure about that. Not after Sophia's bout with... something... on Samhain evening. He couldn't remember. "They're bait. I know. Answer my questions. Which way? How far ahead are they?"

She held up her hand as if she were listening for something.

Back in Alfheim, Bjorn had zapped him with a spell to clear away his fatigue. Which it had. But he was pretty sure the shortness of temper that always happened when he needed sleep was still there. Still festering. Still making him hotheaded.

That hotheadedness was what had gotten him into his original vampire problem.

She looked around. "We need a plan," she said.

Ah, yes, he thought. *Our best-laid plans.*

Wrenn shook her head, then peered into the trees again. "I don't see where they are," she said. "Ranger's not actively spiking his magic. I think I hear Red."

The sword was still talking to her. "What's it saying? Is it aware that it's with my kids?" Because the *other* magical artifact seemed well aware when it was around children.

"She keeps repeating 'We bind thee, Fenrir.' I can track her, but she's not stable enough to help." Wrenn snatched a good-sized branch off the ground. "So we need a plan, especially if we run into vampires." She twirled it around her hand. "Will one of these work on the local vamps if I use it as a stake?"

Fenrir, he thought. "Fenrir?" he asked.

Fenrir meant Ragnarok.

And Ragnarok meant an end to the elves.

He didn't know that for sure. But then again, most people who got a cancer diagnosis didn't know *for sure* that it was going to kill them. Who knew? You might get hit by a bus instead.

"Fenrir," he sighed. Ragnarok was going to kill him. He was pretty sure of it. "I need to get my kids." Get them home and make plans to keep his family as safe as possible during the end of the world.

The expression on Wrenn's face suggested that she was a lot better at reading people than her brother. It also suggested that she was a lot better at making sure other people didn't read her. "You do understand that if this leads to one of us—or Ranger, for that matter—killing Warren Clayton, there's going to be a war."

Ed sighed again. "From my understanding, the kelpies thought they could profit off the vamp-on-vamp violence that's already going on." He pushed his way into the brush again. "As a great man once said, 'Let them fight.'"

The faster the dark magicals killed each other off, the fewer of them they'd have to deal with post-Ragnarok. If there was going to be a post-Ragnarok.

"They're kidnapping regular fae and feeding them to the vampires," Wrenn said.

"That damned kelpie kidnapped my regular *kids* and he's about to feed *them* to the vampires!" Ed shouted.

Whatever Bjorn had done to counter his fatigue hadn't propped up the mechanisms he used to keep his hotheadedness under control.

Probably because that control came from a lot of what his wife called metacognition.

Wrenn peered at Ed's eyes. "Bjorn Thorsson's anti-fatigue spell is wearing off." She didn't ask. She stated.

"You think, Victorsdottir?"

Her jaw clenched. "I was on the brink of drowning. Victor found me. He made sure I didn't die." She blinked three, four times in rapid succession. "He told me I couldn't leave because he'd built a *monster* and that *monster* wanted me as his mate."

"And?" Ed asked. She was big and strong and could have smacked the living shit out of that fop he'd seen in the Heartway so she was running on excuses.

Her lip twitched. "You're his friend, aren't you?"

"Who?" he responded, though he knew damned well who she meant.

"The monster."

Ed laughed. "You believed what Victor Frankenstein told you?"

"He tried to drown me." Her voice had turned ice cold.

Ed blinked. "Victor tried to drown you? I thought you said he'd saved you."

She looked as if she was about to throw a punch. "Your *friend* tried to drown me," she spat through clenched teeth.

And there it was. The railroad connecting two hundred years of Wrenn Goodfellow's beliefs contained a hub of fakery around which she'd built a good chunk of her life. Was it Ed's job to rip down the façade? Maybe. Maybe not. But he was a hothead, and like she said, Frank was his friend.

"You think *Frank* tried to drown you?" He laughed again. "Frank, who has lived with the elves since that ice thing with your fa—Victor Frankenstein? Frank's a teddy bear." A preoccupied teddy bear, but still a teddy bear.

"His name is Frank?" she asked.

Had she calmed down? "Yes," he answered. "He *did not* try to drown you, Wrenn of the fae. I will stake my reputation on that." Of course he didn't know *for sure* if it was a lie. How could he? But he had a pretty good sense of human behavior. "Do you really think the elves of Alfheim would have adopted a murderer?"

She rolled her eyes.

He realized immediately the hypocrisy of his statement. "Those two vampires were an experiment. The elves wanted to see if they could help them be better. They did, for seventy years. Then..." He waved his hand toward the coast. "The point is that we all knew what those two vampires were, but the elves, they had to try. We all know what Frank is, too. There's no need to try, with him."

Her lips thinned. "I have Victor's notes. His logs. I have proof."

Ed threw his hands into the air. "Did the fae get those for you?" She sure was holding on tight to those beliefs, wasn't she? "Because something tells me you're firmly under the thumb of your precious King Oberon."

She pushed by him. "I have a kelpie to bring in."

"A kelpie who just happened to help you steal an elven artifact that's talking up *Ragnarok*, for Odin's sake! And drops you into *Alfheim*? Where your brother Victor told you is a monster just happens to live? Right after we have a *fae problem*?" A fae problem that probably involved Frank in the first place.

Ed pushed by Wrenn. "You are being played," he said. Fae always played. "Stay away from my kids!" he roared. The elves were enough. He didn't need his own fae problem.

A whooping roar echoed between the walls.

A helicopter.

No lights were visible in the sky, and with the trees muffling and distorting sound, Ed had no way to tell where the copter was. It wasn't nearby, that was for sure. "That sounded about a mile away," he said.

Wrenn climbed up into a hollow in the old mission's walls. She tested the adobe on either side, chose the west side, and jumped for the broken top of the wall.

"What are you doing?" he asked.

She hung from the side of the wall, now a good seven feet off the ground, and hand-over-handed her way toward the taller, sturdier corner of the old building. "I might be able to see Ranger's magic from up here."

Or that damned sword. "I think it came from the east." Which meant the coast.

Wrenn's hand slipped. Pebbles dropped to the dirt. She kicked her foot into the adobe as if she were digging into a cupcake.

"Careful," Ed said.

"Yes, Dad," she responded as she pulled herself up to the top of the broken adobe wall.

Wrenn crouched a good fifteen feet up on the old mission's corner like some black clad superhero. She gripped the wall with one hand and shielded her eyes from the starlight with the other.

The copter's engine shutting down echoed through the area.

"There!" She pointed due east, toward the coast, as he suspected. "Lights. Magic, too."

Ed hopped up on the hollow and did his best to see over the trees. There was definitely a glow that hadn't been there a moment ago.

"There's a helicopter!" Wrenn jumped the full fifteen feet down from the wall. She landed, skipped, and rolled like some parkour jumper who knew exactly what they were doing. "Try to keep up, lawman," she said, and darted into the trees.

She'd outstrip him with her longer legs even if he kept pace. "I'm the one with the gun!" he called.

She didn't even look back.

He'd pissed her off with his comments about Frank and Victor Frankenstein. Here he was in the scrub brush in a South Texas wildlife reserve with a fae version of Frank Victorsson—because she was Frank's sister, no matter how much she wanted to argue about it—and he'd made her mad enough that she'd left him behind.

CHAPTER 23

G abe Martinez wasn't sure when the kelpie turned into a
stallion. He wasn't sure how he or Sophie got onto his back,
either, or how the sword had gotten all tangled up with the leather
and rings of the kelpie's bridle.

Ranger had touched the sword and a wave had blasted off it like a
big thick-walled bubble. Then they were moving, even though they
weren't—like Ranger and the sword had loaded the van, and the floor,
and the garage door, and the snowblower all on a flatbed truck like
the ones they use to film actors driving cars. It was all fake. Moving,
yet not, and someone else was in control.

It wasn't Ranger, either. Or the sword. Then Gabe blinked and
they weren't in the van anymore. They were on Ranger's back
galloping toward the coast and the beach and the sand.

Sophia held tight to Gabe's waist. She buried her face in his t-shirt
and mumbled things he couldn't hear. The sword glowed in real,
visible light. Gabe coiled Ranger's mane around his hands and held on
with all his strength, and prayed his sister would do the same.

He'd promised Momma he'd keep her safe.

Ranger dropped into a trot and picked his way down the grass-
covered slopes to the sands of a beach. The moon shimmered just

above the horizon and cast a long trail of silver over the ocean. Waves lapped on the beach. Something howled in the distance. And two bubbles of town light glowed not too far away—the closer of the two to the north and the larger, more distant, glow to the south.

Gabe had no idea where they were other than on a beach someplace a lot warmer than Minnesota. It could be California, or Florida, or somewhere in South America, for all he knew. But he didn't think so.

"South Texas," Sophia said.

They were on the Gulf Coast. The glow to the north was probably South Padre Island.

"The ocean stinks," Sophia said.

The Gulf of Mexico smelled pretty much the same as the California beaches—sandy and sour and like water you should never drink. Some people liked the smell, but Gabe found it gross. Lake Superior smelled big and full of living things, too, except Lake Superior didn't smell like someone had left a salted dead turtle to rot in the sun.

Maybe the stink wasn't the water. Maybe it was the kelpie.

"Ranger smells like a dead seahorse," Sophie said.

Between the *s* at the start of "seahorse" and the *s* at the end, they dropped from the back of a huge stallion onto their butts in the sand.

Ranger, now back in his black kilt and with the sword in his hand, stood over them. "I smell like my loch, missy," he drawled. "Love ye too, by the bye." He squatted and peered at both of them as if to check that they were still pristine and tasty for the vampires. "Either o' ye move an inch an' I'll slice you up, aye?"

Sophia leaned toward him. "Tell the truth, Ranger," she said.

He sighed and rubbed at his face with his free hand. Then he looked over his shoulder at the glow that had to be South Padre Island. "Th' vampires will be here soon." He nodded toward the brush in the direction they'd ridden in from. "They watch for activity at tha' Heartway gate. They ken somethin' yummy's come through for their wee appetites." He frowned. "Children are a delicacy, it seems. 'Nother reason they like bein' this close t' the border." He nodded south. Then he groaned. "I should send ye in wi' th' sword an' instructions on how t' make it go boom again."

Gabe opened his mouth to ask about the sword, but Sophia touched his arm and shook her head. She wanted Ranger to talk.

"So ye think I'm gonnae do th' villain monologue thing? Tell ye my plans, is that it?" He rubbed his face again. "Should be obvious to ye two, bein' th' smartlings ye are."

"Trading us won't save your life," Sophia said.

He chuckled.

"Why didn't you go home?" Gabe asked. "You could have, right? When you brought us here through that gate? Why didn't you leave us behind and vanish?" He was selfish enough.

Ranger stood and looked back at the island. "I broke th' Queen's code," he said. "Me an' my two brothers, we left th' stables durin' th' ruckus, an' instead of respondin' t' th' Queen's call, we visited th' King's castle." He rubbed his face again. "My brothers would do anythin' I told 'em to do." He sniffed and snorted. "Not too bright, those two."

"You're the smart one," Sophia said.

Gone was the defiance she'd had when she'd called him a moron back at the house, like she actually meant what she said. Ranger was the "smart one" in all this.

He laughed. "I'm th' *old* one." He looked Gabe over. "I'm gonnae give ye a boon, my intelligent young friend."

Gabe raised his hands. "No deals!"

Ranger's eyes narrowed. "A boon is freely given. If ye dinnae want it, that's yer problem." He nodded toward Sophia. "I'll give it to Miss Ne'er-the-oracle over here instead."

"We decline all gifts from the fae!" Gabe said. He didn't want to come out of this owing a kelpie a favor. If they survived.

"There aren't that many o' us left." Ranger ignored Gabe and tapped his chest. "Us kelpies. We... fell out o' favor. Now we all live in th' Queen's stables." He sighed. "No matter how any o' us bluster about how we're gonnae take yer lakes, we cannae. King's orders." He rubbed his forehead this time. "I hope the Queen shows my brothers mercy." He looked down at Sophia as if asking her for confirmation.

"I'm not an oracle," she said.

He rubbed the tip of his nose. "No, ye aren't, are ye? But ye know who is."

"Yes," she said.

He nodded. "Tell her I tried."

"I will."

He nodded again. "Goin' home isnae an option, nae when I'm wanted by th' Royal Guard for crimes against the King. So I'm permanently on the lam, as they say." He chuckled and waved at the universe. "Ye want the truth, eh?" He squatted next to Sophia again. "How important is the truth right now, Miss Ne'er-the-oracle?"

Slowly Sophia reached out, and just as slowly, she touched his face. "Maybe you *are* worthy."

Ranger laughed. "My kind will ne'er again be allowed such power an' ye ken that, Ne'er-the-oracle."

Sophia shrugged.

Whooping echoed off the water and individual lights over the glow grew distinct.

A helicopter approached.

Ranger stood. He spun the sword around his wrist before sticking it into the sand. "The plan." He winked at Gabe. "The vamps give me control o' th' fae side o' th' arrangements an' I give them ye two as compensation. They stop feedin' on my few remainin' brothers an' return to th' old ways o' feedin' on only those we provide." He inhaled, then exhaled slowly. "Vampires can fight amongst themselves all they want, but no more riskin' Titania an' Oberon."

Sophia squeezed Gabe's arm again.

Ranger looked down at Gabe as the copter approached and whipped up the air. "Now ye keep the young lady here while I talk to Mr. Clayton, understand? Ye're mundanes. Dinnae run an' cause th' vamps t' chase ye. They cannae help themselves when there's prey." He winked again. "Neither can I."

The copter landed about a hundred feet down the beach and the door slid open. Two men jumped out—one wearing a huge cowboy hat, a suit, and cowboy boots with spurs, and the other dressed in all-black commando gear. A female vampire with huge balloon-like breasts, lips so red they were obvious from where Gabe and Sophia sat on the beach, huge fake-blonde hair, shoes with deadly-looking heels, and a glittery red sequin dress waited in the copter. She chewed gum, checked her spikey nails, and looked bored.

Ranger sniffed the air. He frowned. "That must have hurt," he muttered. "Since I took her token." Then he shrugged and walked toward the vampires.

He didn't mean the weird female vampire in the copter. He hadn't been looking at her.

Had the tall woman Gabe didn't know, the one who'd reached for the van's door handle, followed them? Had the elves? "Is Papa here?" he asked Sophia, even though there was no way Papa could have found them.

She grinned.

If Papa had followed, then other magicals were here.

Hopefully they'd get here before the vamps decided to have a snack.

CHAPTER 24

R anger said something to the vampire in the big hat, then pointed at Gabe and Sophia. Big Hat nodded and shooed Commando in their direction.

Gabe pulled his sister to his side. If they ran, the vampire would catch and eat them for sure. If they stayed, the vampires would probably pass them around like a bowl of candy.

"Are they here, Sophia?" he whispered. "Are they coming?"

"Don't talk to the vampire," she said, and pushed away from his grip. Then she settled herself on the grass like she was about to talk to an Eternal One in a video game.

The bodyguard Commando vamp stopped about six feet from Gabe and Sophia. He stood with hands clasped in front of his groin the way all commandos stood, dressed head-to-toe in black tactical gear like he was an action movie star. Black glasses covered his eyes even though all they had out here was starlight. Black driving gloves covered his hands. His long-sleeved tactical t-shirt showed off his bodybuilder physique, but his pale, uncovered skin still glowed in the night air like someone had polished up a stick of chalk.

He had one of those military knock-off guns Papa hated so much.

The kind that killed a lot people in a very short amount of time and made Papa's job so unsafe, even in Alfheim.

It was like these vampires had forgotten how to fake being mundane and were walking around wearing clown outfits because someone on the Internet told them that was how real people dressed.

Sophia stared at the guard. "He's going to kill you the moment he doesn't think he needs his personal army anymore." She pointed at the Ten Gallon vamp talking to Ranger. "Once he's in control, he's going to behead you and your entire crew."

"Sophia!" Gabe whispered. "Leave the vampire alone." The last thing they needed was to egg on a vampire.

The bodyguard's lip twitched.

"Did he tell you who we are?" she asked the vamp. "You never liked Mr. Oil Man's son, did you? No one liked him. He was dangerous even to your kind. Messed up in the head like..." Her eyebrows pinched together. "... like an old coyote who'd been feeding on garbage too long."

How did she know so much?

"You were in on ignoring him, weren't you? Part of the team that let him slip his leash and go eat people like us."

The bodyguard's lip twitched again.

Sophia's eyes widened. "You all did it on purpose hoping the elves would come down from the north and take care of your problem for you! And now you all act like my papa didn't do you a favor."

The guard did a little *Heh* movement with his shoulders and eyebrow.

Sophia pointed at the vamp but turned to Gabe. "They eat college kids who come here to party."

Not that Gabe knew anything about South Padre Island, other than that it was where several of the Gulf Coast Clans ran tourist businesses, and that they were never, ever to come down here for any reason whatsoever, now or in the future.

At least that's what Momma told Papa one night when they thought all the kids were either playing or asleep. She'd said something about asking the elves to "deal with the problem once and for all," and Papa had responded with something about the vampires being "slave runners before the Civil War. There's money and heritage involved."

It still didn't make any sense why the vampires had been allowed to run businesses in South Padre Island. In Alfheim, the elves always "took care of the problem." Except for their own vampires. And look how that had turned out.

Ten Gallon pointed at the sword, then raised his hands. Seemed these bloodsuckers didn't want anything around that would give the elves an excuse to come around again.

Sophia stared at the sword. "The elves don't care about you, Mr. Vampire."

The guard moved his head to look down at her, but he didn't say anything.

"They care about *us*," Gabe said. "So you know. Even if your boss leaves that sword in the dirt, the elves *definitely* have an excuse to pay you all a visit."

"Mr. Bjorn was *soooo maaaddddd*, wasn't he, Gabe?" Sophia asked. "And Ms. Benta can be mean but she likes Momma a lot and Ranger there hurt our momma who's about to have another baby." She inhaled. "And that made Ms. Benta *soooo maaaddddd*." She shook her head.

"Sophia..." Gabe whispered.

"I tell the truth, Gabe!" she said. "It's going to be like that television show about the Vikings but with magic and a lot of dead vampires." She scrunched up her little face. "I bet Mr. Magnus would be happy to buy all the resorts here. Papa says he's a good businessman."

"*Sophia!*" She'd told him not to talk to the vampire but here she was poking him with a stick.

Sophia leaned toward the guard. She twisted her head to the side. "Do you have a plan?"

The vampire gave her a little nod.

She leaned back and cupped her hands over her mouth. "He has *a plan*, Gabe!" she shout-whispered.

Behind them, in the clearing in front of the copter, Ten Gallon gave Ranger a little shove. Ranger responded by swinging the sword around and pointing it at Ten Gallon's head.

The bodyguard sighed. He stripped off his black-lensed glasses.

His eyes were so blue and bright they looked like ice from a glacier. "Darlin'," he drawled. "I suppose those elves of yours don't know nothin' about American Chosen One lore, huh? 'Cause they ain't real Americans." He snorted. "I should kill you now and save myself some future agony. But where'd the fun be with that?"

Ten Gallon laughed as Ranger backed away.

"What's your name?" Sophia asked the vampire.

"Oh, sweetie pie, I'm Faceless Thug Number One." He turned away from them so fast Gabe didn't see him move. He placed three shots into Ten Gallon's head, and another three into his heart.

Sophia screamed.

"He shoulda realized when I didn't heed The Call that I was a threat," the vamp said.

Ranger, sword in hand, ran for the bushes. The shots got the female vamp's attention, but not so much that she stopped looking bored. The pilot sat behind the controls and didn't seem to notice what was happening.

The bodyguard pulled a machete off his back as he walked toward Ten Gallon. "Run along, lil' Chosen Ones, before I change my mind."

Gabe grabbed his sister and they ran as fast as they could into the trees.

CHAPTER 25

The copter lifted off just as Ed and Wrenn burst through the brush. Ed's shotgun wouldn't do damage, not twenty yards down the beach, nor was it likely to even nick the paint on that particular machine. The thing was as black as the night and looked fully shielded.

"You're a witch!" he shouted. "Zap it or something!" Not that he believed she was a witch any more than he believed Frank Victorsson was a jotunn.

But they had to do something. His kids were on that copter.

"I'm not a strong witch!" Wrenn threw a rock at the copter as it lifted into the air. "That kind of intervention takes a full magical." She pulled out her phone and waved it at Ed. "We can call in the Guard."

There'd be repercussions if either the elves or the fae showed up in South Padre Island and engaged the vampires in a full-frontal attack.

But then again, Ragnarok was upon them, so as the kids said, you only live once. "Do *not* call in the fae." He pulled out his phone. Magnus's number went to voicemail. "If you can do the whole gate thing, now's the time," he said. He hung up and dialed Bjorn and left the same message.

"They're on their way," Wrenn said.

She had no idea. None. "How the hell do you know that?" he yelled.

"Because they're not fae—quiet." She held up her hand. "Red?"

They hadn't taken the sword? Ed turned around to look back into the brush, in the direction Wrenn had pointed her ear even though she was looking down so she could concentrate.

He turned, and Ranger punched him in the face.

"I *dinnae* like ye, mundane," the kelpie said.

Ed stepped back and swung up the shotgun. "Where are my children?" The son of a bitch had to know.

Ranger also stepped back and swung up the sword. "Ye managed t' scuttle my chances here an' ye did it wi'out even bein' on th' beach."

Ed cocked the gun. "Did they take my kids?" Maybe the kids had run into the brush. "Gabe! Sophia!" They needed to stay hidden and away from the kelpie, but Ed needed to know.

Ranger flicked back and forth between pointing the sword at Ed and pointing it at Wrenn. "Clayton's dead," he said. "His douchey bodyguard macheted that hat right off his ten-gallon head." He used his other hand to draw a line over the braided leather and silver around his neck.

"So?" Ed said. Vamp-on-vamp violence wasn't his problem.

"So?" Ranger chuckled. "Old clan dead. New clan doesnae care." He shrugged.

Were he and his family free of the vampire threat? Ed aimed the gun. "Where are my kids?" he yelled.

"Queen Titania's gonnae make an example o' me," Ranger said. "If I go back. She might even hand me over t' the King first, so he can make his own example."

"Help me take down the entire syndicate and I'll ask the King to give you leniency," Wrenn said. She moved closer.

"An' then I'd be a traitor t' my kind, a kelpie who helped a woman o' my own free will." Ranger slid his foot back as if he were about to run into the brush.

If he dropped into stallion form, they'd never catch him.

"Alfheim will help you," Ed said. He shouldn't offer Alfheim's magical help to anyone or anything. Ever. It wasn't his place. Or his pay grade. "They helped Tony and Ivan for seventy years until they turned on the elves." And they would have stayed helped, if Frank's brother hadn't come around.

"Nae thanks, lawman. I'd rather not trade th' Queen's golden cage for one lined wi' elven silver."

Ed lowered the shotgun. It always came back to cages, didn't it? His. The kids'. The *elves'*, for goodness sake, that one huge cage where they were trapped by the ways of their mundanes because that's how magic worked. They were as naively insular and stoic as the local Nordic Americans, because for the elves, it was literally as genetic as it was cultural.

And everyone inside that cage had to deal with its bars every single day.

But the elves were trying. It was like eating healthy when every single one of your genes screamed *I'm gonna explode your heart and kill ya early*. Hence the mistakes with the vampires.

And here Ed was offering up a new sacrifice to that very same mistake by promising a kelpie access to the same floundering attempt at expanding their horizons that had let vampires into Alfheim in the first place.

What the hell was wrong with him? No kelpies in Alfheim.

"You think you're in a cage?" Ed yelled. "What'd you do to get yourself locked up, Dumbass McHorseface? Huh? Besides all the murdering and trafficking and dark fae-ing? You know, the behaviors that should get you put down, not locked up?" He aimed the shotgun again.

For a split second, Ranger's face fell as if he were a kid who'd just realized how terrible he was for kicking the dog. But that look vanished as quickly as it had appeared and the kelpie's face stretched out into that terrified crazy look of manic fury.

"Ranger…" Wrenn held out her hand. "Give me the sword."

He glared at her. "I remember this sword," he growled.

Wrenn dropped her hand. "What?"

"She remembers me," he said. "Why d' ye think I can hold her?

Why d' ye think she keeps callin' out about bindin' Fenrir?"

"Set. It. Down, Ranger," Wrenn said. *"Now."*

"Tell me where my kids are!" Ed yelled. "Did the vamps take them?"

"Dinnae ken! Dinnae care, lawman!" Ranger bellowed.

"I've killed a vamp," Ed snarled. "I'll kill a kelpie, too."

"Oh, aren't we manly!" Ranger made a kissy face. "Perhaps ye *are* like-minded."

"Stop!" Wrenn yelled.

She pointed at the brush about twenty feet down the beach.

Sophia stood on the sand, her brother behind her with his hand on her shoulder. "We ran when the vampires..." She inhaled. "The one shot the other one with the hat."

"Then he used a machete, Papa. Sophia didn't see," Gabe said.

Which meant *he* had. He'd seen a vampire behead another vampire. In real life, under a Texas moon, on a real beach.

Ed's kids knew his job sometimes involved bad things, and that sometimes those bad things were horrible and terrifying and that they gave both Momma and Papa bad dreams.

But they didn't have specifics about the bad things. They thought violence meant hitting your sibling and him saying *Ow!* They thought breaking the law meant a stern talking-to from someone in a brown Alfheim County Sheriff Department uniform.

The vast majority of his job *was* issuing warnings and directing traffic. But sometimes there were vampires. Sometimes there were kelpies. And sometimes there were fae problems that meant his kids saw things they should not.

"That sword would have killed you the first time you met, Ranger," Sophia said. "She'll do it now, the moment she fully wakes up."

Or knew things they should not.

Ranger looked at the sword in his hand. His mouth rounded.

He dropped the blade.

The hotheaded, exhausted part of Ed's brain wanted to use the butt of his shotgun to beat Ranger into unconsciousness. To take care of the problem once and for all, even though he doubted he could do enough real damage to the kelpie to... what? Curb-stomp his brain into the sand? Incapacitate him? Haul him into a holding cell in Alfheim?

This wasn't the same as the situation with the vampire. Ranger wasn't actively attacking him. Nothing about Ed's past mattered in relation to a kelpie who trafficked fae victims, except the victims part.

He shouldered the gun again. "On your knees. Hands on your head. Now!"

Ranger looked at Sophia. "I hope ye survive this, young one."

White magical fire flared out from the sides of Ranger's eyes like he was some cartoon character. Blistering white light, as if the brightness itself would cause wounds and welts.

And then it was gone and his eyes were back to their ice green.

Wrenn knocked him to the ground and dropped her full body weight onto his back, pinning his hips and arms. "The bridle," she said. "On his neck. Get it off."

Ed remembered something about kelpies and their bridles. He pulled out his pocketknife and flipped open the blade.

"Dinnae cut it!" Ranger wailed. "Please. Dinnae."

Ed looked at the knots and braids as they wove themselves through the multiple silver rings. "What do I do?" he asked.

"I will find that fine wife of yours," Ranger growled through a thickening accent. "I cannot help myself. *I am a kelpie.*"

A wrong accent. He sounded somewhere between Latin and Spanish.

The next string of words was not Scottish, or any Spanish Ed understood, though he knew the kelpie spoke Spanish. He picked out words that sounded very much like *life* and *church*.

The white fire around Ranger's eyes reappeared.

"What the hell?" Ed's instincts were to get away from the kelpie. To move back as far as possible. To not breathe the same air.

He cut off the bridle and yanked it out from around Ranger's neck.

The kelpie immediately calmed down. The white vanished. Ranger coughed and inhaled sharply. "I must do as ye order, lawman," he whispered. "Ye have my bridle."

A thought manifested in Ed's head. A terrible thought, one he would never admit to anyone. One that came out because of his exhaustion, and his hotheadedness.

Tell him to kill himself, he thought. Sweep away the problem, out of his thoughts and out of his life. To be judge, jury, and executioner as if he were as much an aspect of a god as his employers.

If it had been just them out here on this beach, he would have. But Wrenn would take Ranger back to where some of those victims might see a tiny bit of justice. And Ed heard shuffling behind them.

"We will take the bridle," Sophia said.

Wrenn put out her hand. "Are you sure you want to keep a kelpie's bridle? You'll have him under control, but not his brothers."

"We're a syndicate, ye ken," Ranger said.

Sophia stared Wrenn dead in the eye, her almost-ten-year-old face stern and her lips set. "Gabe, put the bridle in your pocket. Please, Papa. It needs to come home with us."

She wanted Ed to give it to her brother. "Can you tell us why, honey?" he asked gently.

She pointed at Ranger and shook her head. "This is the oracle's boon to you," she said.

She knew exactly what she was saying, and why, and for whom. Of this Ed was sure. He handed the bridle to Gabe, who stuffed it into his pocket.

"Looks like my daughter wants the Alfheim Sheriff's Department to be in charge of your life, Ranger." He stood and backed away with his kids.

Sophia blinked. She inhaled. Then she hugged his waist. "Papa!" She hiccupped as if this were the first time during the entire ordeal she'd allowed herself to be afraid. "I don't like Texas. I want to go home to Minnesota."

He did, too. To his wife. To their new baby. To his annoying job he liked and to the annoying locals he mostly liked, except for the many random mouthy Brad Andersons. To the good schools and the clean air.

And the traffic accidents that always banged up expensive cars but never did hurt drivers beyond a bruise or two.

It was a cage, yes, but Ed was pretty sure the door was unlocked.

He still needed to figure out how dangerous the outside world was.

Now to get them home. "Sweetie," he knelt down to give her a hug, "we'll go home."

Wrenn pulled Ranger to his feet. "Back to the station," she said. "You pay the toll this time."

He chuckled.

"Answer Wrenn Goodfellow's questions thoroughly and truthfully," Ed called. "And do as she says. Don't cause more problems or inflame the ones you've caused already."

Ranger stuck out his tongue.

Sophia stuck her tongue right back at him.

"I'm gonnae miss ye, my lovely Ne'er-the-oracle."

She gave him the finger.

"Sophia!" Ed said. "Young lady!"

She shrugged. "Kelpies are evil, Papa."

Wrenn pushed him into the brush. "I suggest leaving that sword right where it is. Let the elves deal with it."

He had no intension of touching the blade. Not now. Not ever.

Gabe, though, seemed quite fascinated. "Leave it alone, son," Ed called.

His boy looked up. "It's glowing."

He said it so nonchalantly that the words didn't immediately register with Ed … sort of like the enchanted sword was supposed to glow, because that's what they did, and it *not* glowing would have been the anomaly.

Except they were mundanes, and they didn't see glowy magic, nor did they feel it. So it should have been just a sword lying in the sand.

A not-glowing sword.

"Gabe!" Ed ran for his son. "Get away from the—"

He ran headfirst into a strange woman wearing an antlered helmet.

CHAPTER 26

W renn knew immediately who had stepped out of one of the many veils and directly into poor Ed's path. Only a handful of fae had that much power, and only one of that particular small subset had the audacity to steal an intelligence dryad's armor off her back and then parade around in it like it was some sort of kid's costume.

Wrenn's boss's wayward wife, the other royal fae with enough raw magical ability to pop in and out of any situation at any time she wanted: Titania, Queen of the Fae, now stood on the sand between Ed and his son.

The Queen showed up on this particular Texas beach in the gloom and all the bloodsucker doom *after* the vampires had probably given Ed's kids deep psychological traumas. After Red had destroyed Ed's house and hurt those werewolves. After the Heartway had cut Wrenn with Victor's ghost.

After how many sprites had been trafficked by Ranger's brothers?

Wrenn swore under her breath. Queen Titania helped only herself, which meant she was about to make this entire situation significantly worse.

Wrenn yanked her Royal Guard star off her belt. "Queen Titania of the Fae!" she called out, more so that Ed would understand just who it was into whom he'd smacked. "I am Wrenn Goodfellow of the Royal Guard. This kelpie is under arrest." She knocked Ranger. "The mundane and his children are under my protection."

Not that her protection would count for much if Titania was in a mood.

Ranger gulped. "I'm sorry, Queen Titania!" he wailed as he fell to his knees. "I didnae heed yer call an' I am so *very* sorry for my misdeeds!"

Under the antlered helmet, the Queen frowned.

"As Royal Guard and the King's Paladin, I serve the fae," Wrenn said. *All of the fae*, Wrenn thought. Not just the royals and their whims.

Because this was about a whim. It had to be. Why else would Titania show up *after* all the fun was over? She was here to collect the spoils for herself.

Which meant someone here was about to pay and no one anywhere would get justice.

Titania's frown turned to a wry grin.

We bind thee, Fenrir! Red called out in an increasingly uneven and pained way.

Wrenn's eye twitched. Part of her wanted to run to the sword and to offer comfort. But all of her understood that Redemption wasn't her problem anymore.

The Queen was.

"I'm here for my stallion," Titania said.

"Yes," Wrenn said. "I figured." She didn't release Ranger.

The Queen pulled off the antlered helmet and tossed it to the side, then thought better of it. "You, Royal Guard woman." She pointed at the helmet. "I need you to take that and this—" She waved her hands disapprovingly over the dryad's armor she wore. "—back to my husband's lackeys."

"I would be happy to do so, my Queen, once I take in this kelpie for processing."

The Queen rolled her eyes. "They're naughty. I know. But we have to give them some leeway or they won't be able to keep their worst behaviors under control. Such is how we contain the dark among us."

Wrenn gave Ranger a shake. "Your stallion is part of a blood syndicate run by the kelpies from your stable," she said. "They've been trafficking victims to the Gulf Coast vampires here in the mundane world." *How is that "naughty"?* she thought. She didn't dare say it out loud. Not to the Queen.

Titania's nonchalant annoyance turned into what looked to Wrenn to be actual concern. "Is that true?" She stared at Ranger. "Answer me."

Yet she obviously knew what the kelpies were doing. Maybe she hadn't realized the true depths of the naughtiness. "An exsanguinated sprite washed up on the banks of the Titan River a few days ago," Wrenn said. Maybe she could get the Queen on board with completely shutting down the syndicate.

Titania's expression changed. She hadn't known about the sprite.

"The vampires turned one of your kelpies," Wrenn said. "Robin Goodfellow dusted him in a tavern's kitchen Samhain evening."

That she *definitely* had not known. Royal anger spread in spikey waves through her red and green magic.

Ranger sniffed. "I wonder what kind o' panic we'd have ourselves if th' regular fae folk kent about vamped kelpies," he drawled.

Titania's eyes narrowed.

The desire to punch the side of Ranger's head almost overcame Wrenn's control. Punch him and haul him down the beach to Red so she could run him through.

We bind thee! Red called.

Because everyone involved would see using an unstable elven sword to end one of the Queen's stallions as justice, right? Even if they did, it wouldn't make good politics.

It'd get Wrenn banished. Or executed.

Titania winced and looked as if she wanted to glance at the sword. Did she hear Red, too?

Ed's boy looked at the sword, then up at Queen Titania, then back at the sword. "Ma'am," he said, "there's a glowing sword and I don't think we should be standing this close to it."

Titania inhaled and the anger abruptly froze. It didn't leave her magic, just stopped spiking.

She smoothed the lovely swirls of her dark blonde hair away from her face. "And who are you, my dear handsome young mundane?"

She knew who she was talking to. Who Ed was, too. She had, for some reason, decided to be polite to Ed's son.

The kid somehow kept his composure. "My name is Gabriel Martinez. It's a pleasure to meet you, Queen Titania of the Fae."

He offered his hand.

Ranger *hmphed*. "The vamps were mutterin' somethin' about American Chosen One lore," he whispered.

Wrenn looked down at the kelpie.

"What?" he said. "I can respect a couple o' bairns if I want tae."

Ed stood there in front of Titania utterly stunned and looking as if he were about to grab his kids and run. Which, honestly, he should have done already.

Titania put her hand on her chest as if Gabriel had just offered her the loveliest pearl in all creation. She leaned toward the kid, then looked at Ed and his Sheriff's Department uniform. "Are you the elves' lawman?" she asked. She slapped her thigh. "You are! And you're his son?" she asked the boy.

He continued to offer his hand. "Yes, Ma'am," he said. "But I think we need to make sure Papa's okay and to move away from the sword."

Good kid, Wrenn thought.

"See?" Ranger said.

Queen Titania looked around the child. "Oh! Ranger, you disobedient boy!" she called as if she'd just noticed the sword. "Did you steal the elves' pointy object?"

"Th' Royal Guard woman did it!" Ranger yelled.

Wrenn gave him a good shove. "Be quiet."

Titania took young Gabriel's hand. "Come, young man, and bring your dear stunned father." She pulled him up the slope, toward Wrenn and Ranger. The kid, still somehow keeping his composure, managed to haul his father up the hill too. The little girl followed. They left Red where she was.

We bind thee!

The Queen winced again as she stopped directly in front of Wrenn. She peered up as if Wrenn had a wart on her chin. "My, my! The resemblance is *uncanny*."

And there it was again, the "resemblance" thing. Wrenn frowned.

Titania shrugged off the rest of the armor to reveal a simple t-shirt and jeans underneath. She looked deceptively like all the pretty mundanes walking around Texas. "Here, son." She handed Gabriel a tiny bit of metal, a ring or a bit of mail from the armor. "That's for you and all your siblings."

"No gifts from the fae," Ed muttered. He rubbed at his head as if running headlong into Titania had caused him actual damage.

"Now, now." Titania stepped forward and kissed his forehead. Magic flared out around them all, then settled down onto Ed and the boy, but dripped off the girl as if it had hit something slippery. "It'll all be okay."

Wrenn saw no enchantments around any of the mundanes. Nothing overtly elven, and nothing newly fae, which meant either they were clean, or the enchantments were so close to their skin and so thin that they weren't visible.

If she had to bet, she'd take the latter.

We bind thee!

Titania winced again. "Paladin," she said, "I will deal with the kelpies."

All those sprites, all the victims—their families needed justice.

Or not. With the fae, justice and revenge were so closely inter-woven that any official acknowledgement of kelpie wrongdoing could easily spin up into house against house, royal against royal, sprite against satyr, and fae taking out their aggressions on the local witches.

Yet they'd been trafficking. "But..." Wrenn said.

Titania held up her hand. "*Diplomacy*, young lady. The totality of this is a delicate situation and none of your business."

"So it's above my pay grade, is it?" She shouldn't be short with the Queen, but sometimes it was difficult to hold in her annoyance.

Titania sighed. "He is not the only kelpie I need to collect this evening." She turned away from Wrenn. "Now gather that horrid armor and make your way back to my husband."

Dare Wrenn argue with the Queen? Damned royals. There were laws and a Royal Guard for a reason. "They're trafficking sprites, Queen—"

The Queen of the Fae grabbed Wrenn's hands. "*I will deal* with it." A spell rolled down the Queen's arms and onto Wrenn's wrists as she spoke. It flared out more blue and purple than any fae magic Wrenn was used to, and coiled itself around her wrists.

"What—"

Titania touched her lips and shook her head. "Make sure you are gone before the elves show up," she said to Wrenn. "No incidents, understand?"

"She has business in Alfheim," Ed said.

Titania laughed. "That she does!" She tapped Wrenn's arm and leaned close to her ear. "Be kind," she whispered. She pulled back and smiled. "Can't happen until morning, anyway, so go home and feed your fishes, my love."

Was she talking about the monster hidden among Alfheim's people? And how did the Queen know about Wrenn's fish?

Titania grabbed Ranger by the scruff of his neck. "I give you a home, a place where you're fed and cared for, and you do this? You're no better than the vampires." She looked at Ed. "Gather your younglings, my dear Sheriff. Time to return you to my favorite handsome Odin elf."

They all vanished. All of them—Ed, his kids, Titania, and Ranger—and left Wrenn alone on the shadowy beach with a dryad's armor and an elven sword stuck in some kind of memory loop.

The two bands of Titania-made magic around her wrists tightened and flattened. And slowly, delicately, they snaked their way in and around the tattoos she already carried. "*Hmm...*" Wrenn said. The

Queen didn't want other fae to see the enchantments she'd left on Wrenn's body.

Had Titania just given her token spells like the others she carried in the tattoos? Why? Was this part of Titania's "delicate situation"? Because everything was part of a delicate situation with the fae. Being Royal Guard helped insulate her from most of the royal posturing, but this? Just how much bigger than a blood syndicate was this? Would Titania deal with the kelpies? Would the trafficking stop? Would the Queen kill Ranger?

But... she couldn't. The kid had his bridle. The Queen of the Fae might have taken him back to his stable but the Martinez family controlled his destiny.

Wrenn chuckled. The little girl really had given that bastard a boon.

She looked up at the sky. How did the elves and Alfheim fit into all of this? She still didn't know if Victor's vampiric monster was somehow involved. Or his other... her brother. She might as well admit it to herself.

She'd always known, really, what "saving her from drowning" meant. She knew. But being a witch got a lot more respect from the fae than being a monster.

But she was a witch. And not a monster. So nothing had changed. Not really. And now she was to "be kind."

She picked up the dryad's armor and draped it over her arm. Should she take the sword back, too?

We bind thee!

But something told her that taking Red into the Heartway right now wasn't smart, especially without a token. The last thing any realm needed was for the Heartway's reflection of Victor Frankenstein to get his hands on an explode-y sword.

Ghosts shouldn't have power, much less a power named Redemption.

Wrenn picked up the helmet and dusted off the sand. The walk back to the old mission should help steel her for another token-less trip.

After all this time, she should be used to the hells of the Heartway. But she should also be used to the flashbacks by now, too, and the jitters that came with them both. Her body panicked and her mind wanted to talk it down and the whole process exhausted her more than the ripping open of her traumas. She could psych herself up all she wanted but a trip back through the Heartway and another round of it poking a lightning rod into her disturbed soul felt heavy.

Maybe she should wait for the elves. Hitch a ride into Brownsville, where she could book a flight to London; there she could buy a token off a fae in the mundane world. But international flights were few and far between right now, with the mundane world so unsettled.

She walked over to Redemption.

The sword really was glowing in real light. "Take a deep breath, my swordly friend. The elves are on their way. They'll help. It'll be okay."

The sword would do as she asked.

"Are you talking to me again?" She had no idea what to make of this elven blade's possessiveness, or their connection. Or even the possibility that she was, in fact, a witch of elven descent.

Which meant she really should deal with her business in Alfheim.

Wrenn rubbed at the tip of her nose and stared out over the water at the glow from South Padre Island. The sudden decrease in overall vamp numbers a month ago had stirred up this trouble. Nature abhorred a vacuum, so now the vampires were in the midst of an internal war that overflowed not only into the fae realms, but into elf territory.

Or, from Ed's reaction, was caused by something in elf territory.

Why did she keep going back to Victor with all this? That somehow Victor Frankenstein's rot had infected everyone's soil and had triggered... whatever this was.

We bind thee, Fenrir!

She looked down at the glowing sword. "I thought you were going to take a breath?" The glow had decreased, at least.

The talk of Fenrir was worrisome considering the all the chaos in both the mundane and magical worlds. And the Queen's refusal to allow Wrenn to deal with the kelpies through normal channels.

Wrenn reached for Red's hilt.

"Stop!" Wrenn yanked back her hand and turned around.

Robin Goodfellow stood about five feet away. "There you are!" He leaped forward and grabbed her by the scruff of the neck. "Time to come home, young lady."

CHAPTER 27

"Papa!"

Sophia was touching Ed's face, as was a lot of cold air.

"Is he okay?" Gabe said. "I figured if we were calm and respectful with the Queen she wouldn't get mad at us. Did it work?" His feet shuffled on what sounded like dirt. "We're in a pit, but I think we're home."

Ed opened his eyes to a black sky and an even blacker pit. Random snowflakes fluttered downward only to be whipped away by a cold wind that thankfully rolled over the pit more than into it. Somewhere nearby, plastic snapped in the wind. They were a good eight or so feet down in a hole. What remained of the garage floor jutted out along the edges of the hole complete with poking, ragged rebar.

They were in fact at the bottom of the hole left when that damned sword nuked his garage.

His son tried to climb up the loose dirt lining the pit.

"Gabe! Careful!" Ed sat up faster than he should have. What the hell had that fae done to him? "Was that the Queen of the Fae?" he muttered. He'd bounced off her armor and...

He really had no idea how to describe what it had done to his head. He'd been there, on the beach, listening to Wrenn and Gabe deal with the actual, honest-to-goodness Queen of the Fae and none of it had processed. The closest he'd ever come to a similar experience was a drunken bender in college from which he remembered moments and images, but didn't really *remember*, and the lack of memory made him feel a type of naked vulnerability he did not like.

He'd never gone drinking like that again, and after Isabella's parents were killed by a drunk driver, he'd stopped drinking even the occasional beer.

Gabe slid back down to Ed and Sophia.

"You two okay?" he asked.

"We were on the beach, now we're home," Sophia said.

Gabe looked around at the pit. "It's like a Terminator time travel bubble," he said.

Ed rubbed his ear. "Don't give the fae ideas." Wrenn did say they were teching it up.

"I'm cold," Sophia said.

Gabe immediately wrapped his arm around his sister. "I can get out. If I jump, I can reach the concrete."

Ed patted at the dirt. He'd had his coat around his waist before he ran headlong into the Queen of the Fae—there, his coat was bunched up to the side of his hip. "Here, honey," he said, and handed it over to his daughter.

Ed fished his phone from his pants pocket. It lit up long enough to tell him its battery was about to die.

"Ranger made us leave our phones in the van, Papa," Gabe said.

Ed fished out Gabe's phone. "I got them." He handed it to his son.

"You found the van?" Gabe took his phone and unlocked the screen.

Ed handed Sophia hers, which she immediately checked.

"We landed in the same place you did. At that old mission." Ed hit the mic button on his radio. At least that battery hadn't died and he could trust his own people. "Tracy, you there?" Hopefully all the veil-crossings and the Heartway-traveling hadn't messed up his gear. He glanced around. Bad enough he'd lost his shotgun.

His radio crackled. "Sheriff?"

"I have the kids. We're in… my driveway." He huddled close to Gabe and Sophia. It really was cold.

"Copy that," Melanie said. She had the early morning shift, which meant that they'd been gone at least a few hours. "Sending someone now."

She didn't seem too freaked out.

"Date and time," Ed said. The last thing they needed was for the Queen of the Fae to think it would be fun to drop them home twenty years after she plucked them off that beach.

Melanie rattled off the date and time. He'd been correct; they'd been gone only a few hours. "I'm making calls," he said. "Out."

"Copy that," Melanie said. "Out."

"I called Mr. Bjorn." Gabe handed over his phone. "The call went to voicemail."

Ed tapped Lennart's number next. Thankfully, he answered.

"I'm at Frank's place. We have Ella and Mateo here. They're safe and asleep," the sleepy Lennart said. "Bjorn, Magnus, and Benta took a plane. They should be heading to a beach? Correct? That was the last place your phone indicated your location."

So three of the elder elves were on their way to get the sword. "The sword should be there still." As long as Wrenn didn't take it, or the fae come back for it. Or the vampires.

A whining electric car pulled up. "Someone's here."

Lennart paused. "It's—"

"Mr. Arne!" Sophia shouted. "Mr. Arne, we're down here!"

Lennart chuckled. "The King will get you to the hospital."

"Hospi—?"

Lennart hung up.

Ed looked at the phone, shook his head, and handed it back to Gabe. They must have kept Isabella overnight.

Footsteps approached.

Arne Odinsson, in full balding-middle-aged-father glamour, looked over the edge of the pit, though the University of Minnesota hat and its big maroon and gold pompom wasn't really doing a good job of disguising his ears. He wore his old black parka with its fur-lined hood and had a couple of blankets in his hand.

"Magnus has the sword," he said. "They're on their way back to the airport in Brownsville and will be home by morning."

Both of Ed's kids looked up at the King of the Alfheim Elves as if to say *Manners, please.*

Damned elves and their myopic view of life. "We're cold but okay down here," Ed said. "Isabella?"

"Is Momma okay?" Sophia asked.

"Everything's fine!" Arne grinned down at the kids. "I have blankets." He held them out as headlights swept the driveway. "Maura's here to take you and Gabe to Frank's place. Akeyla's up and waiting for you. She said she's going to make hot cocoa." He knelt down and whipped his hands around like he was going to zap them with a spell. "I'm going to cushion the edge here because it's dark and I want to make sure we get you out safely, honey," he said.

Sophia nodded. "Thank you, Mr. Arne."

"Run up the side as fast as you can," Arne said.

Sophia looked up at Ed.

"Go on, honey. Mr. Arne will catch you." The elves always caught them.

Sophia stepped back and shot up the side of the pit farther and faster than she would have been able to without the spell. Arne plucked her from midair and swung her around out of Ed's sight. "Your mommy's water broke, so I'm going to take your daddy to the hospital, okay? Take the blanket and go to Maura, sweetie," he said.

Sophia jogged away from the pit.

"Isabella's water broke?" Ed called.

Gabe made it to the top of the pit wall pretty much on his own. He disappeared out of view too, presumably on his way to Maura's sedan.

"Sif's with her. We should go." Arne extended his hand to Ed.

"We had a run-in with the Queen of the Fae," Ed called up. "You don't see any unwelcomed magicks, do you?" He didn't want to accidentally take nasty fae magicks into Alfheim's hospital.

Arne shook his head. "You're clean," he said.

Ed inhaled and ran at the slope. The spell somehow gave the dirt grip, and did blunt the sharpness of the concrete and the rebar. Arne took his hand and hauled him back into the real world.

Someone had put plastic over the gaping hole in the side of Ed's house and sealed off the entire area with crime scene tape.

Both his kids were at the end of the driveway, being checked over by Arne's daughter, Maura.

Arne turned his back to Maura and the kids. "I asked Titania to bring you home."

Ed gaped at the elf. "Excuse me?" he said reflexively. Elves and fae working together? And then telling Ed, a mere mundane? "You *what?*" This could not be good.

Arne looked annoyed by Ed's shock. "We do not have a Heimdall elder elf here. We cannot manipulate space as easily as the fae and we felt it important that you have magical backup as fast as possible." He sighed. "The deal did not concern you or your children."

Yes it did. She'd showed up on that beach specifically to help them. "Arne…"

Arne stared at the hole in the house. "It was worth it. A man should not miss the birth of his child." Then the Elf King of Alfheim gripped Ed's shoulder and turned back toward Maura and the kids. "Magnus thinks we should build you a new house," he said. "We could ward and charm it properly, plus get you enough bedrooms, now that you are seven. Might take an extra few months, since it's winter."

Ed picked up the last blanket and wrapped it around his shoulders. He didn't care about the house. Not right now.

Sophia and Gabe waved from next to Maura's sedan.

Ed waved back. "I'll call when I know!" he said.

Gabe helped his sister into the car. Maura waved and drove them away, toward Frank Victorsson's lake and hopefully a safe place to rest, at least for the night.

"I think Gabe's going to need to talk to someone," Ed said. "He saw a vampire beheading." He looked at Arne. "I don't think he's processed it yet."

"*Hmm.*" Arne watched Maura and the kids drive away. "Okay."

Gabe will be fine, Ed thought. He didn't know why he felt that way, but he was pretty sure it was true. "We need to talk about Sophia," he said.

Arne nodded. "We do." He ushered Ed toward his car. "Everything will be okay."

Arne's inflection said he didn't believe his own words—and that he probably didn't realize that he didn't believe his words.

Ed didn't argue, or ask more questions, or give Arne more information. He was too tired. "I need coffee." And his wife needed him.

"All right," Arne Odinsson said. "Let's get you to where you need to be, my friend."

CHAPTER 28

Wrenn Goodfellow blinked awake inside a brilliantly warm ray of golden sunshine. The lovely cut glass doors to her left cast brilliant rainbows across the multifaceted parquet of flooring under the mat on which she lay.

She was in Robin's practice room and in the sun, which meant that Robin had moved her back into Oberon's Castle from the beach in Texas. It also meant that she'd lost the rest of the night and probably most of the morning for no discernible reason beyond that it somehow benefited Robin.

At least this time he'd put a pillow under her head.

She sat up. No dryad armor, so he'd dealt with that. No sword, either. "Did you leave Redemption for the elves?" she said into the air.

He was here, hiding behind a glamour between the rainbows, probably bored and angry that she'd stolen his morning fun even though knocking her out and leaving her in the practice room was his doing.

He manifested out of a shaft of sunlight in the corner, still in his midnight blue uniform, still in his preferred young-male and tiny-nubbed glamour, staring at the phone in his hand as if the fate of the universe rested on his ability to win this round of Words with Friends.

His eyebrow arched as he swiped through something on his screen. "*Hmmm...*" he said. "Useful."

"Robin," Wrenn said.

He still didn't look at her.

She snapped her fingers.

He looked up. He frowned. Then he swiped one last time and put the phone inside his jacket. "I returned the armor," he said.

"Thank you." Wrenn stood and stretched her back. "The sword?"

He shrugged. "Did you know that enclave has a Freyr *and* a Freya elder elf? Plus that big burly Thor elf!" He threw his hands into the air. "They're fully stocked, pantheon-wise." He shrugged. "Almost."

She'd been in the presence of the Freya and Thor elder elves, plus another Thor elf and one named Sif who she was pretty sure wasn't a Sif aspect. They'd talked about one named Magnus and their King, whose name, if she remembered correctly, was Arne Odinsson.

So yeah, the North American elven enclave was probably quite well stocked with aspects of the Norse pantheon.

Robin hadn't answered her question. "Do they have the sword?"

He shrugged again. "The Freyr, Freya, and Thor elder elves scooped it up off the beach, if that's what you're asking."

His evasiveness meant she wasn't going to get a straight answer. Not right now, and likely not in the practice room, which meant the politics she'd hoped to avoid were here. Those same politics were probably why she'd lost the rest of the night and most of the morning.

She walked over to his sunbeam. The golden light hit the side of her face and she instinctively turned toward the sun to warm her cold flesh. "Are you going to clue me in?" she asked.

"You will receive guidance on how to word your final report, yes," Robin said. "No need to be alarmist." He sighed and tossed her a *What can I do?* look.

He could do a lot. *He* could tell her the truth so that she didn't accidently get caught up in something that might be dangerous not only to the fae she was supposed to protect, but to her personally.

Or to Ed and his kids, because this was clearly a delicate situation in need of diplomacy, as the Queen had been kind enough to tell her.

The Queen had also showed up *after* Red started calling out about Fenrir.

And here Robin was telling her not to alarm anyone.

Two hundred years of living with the fae and she'd always believed she'd earned enough respect from Robin and King Oberon, the Royal Guard, her neighbors—all of the fae, to be honest—that they wouldn't play with her work. Daily stuff, she expected. The fae were fae, and they were as confined in their ways as every other magical. But the big stuff? Cases that involved murders and trafficking and vampires? *Naughty* was one thing. *Evil* was a whole new level.

Malfeasance, she thought.

Did she trust the Queen to actually deal with the kelpies? Or was she to be quiet about the vampires feeding on fae and an elven sword calling out about Fenrir and a secretive, powerful elven enclave living in North America?

"I hear it's been unseasonably cold in some of the Queen's realms," Robin said. "Like winter stayed all summer."

Yes, let's not be alarmist. Or help anyone prepare. "It's been the opposite in the mundane world," she said. "Hot and full of plagues."

Robin slapped his goat knee. "Strange how that works." He leaned in close to her ear. "I cleaned up all the messes while you slept. Go home. Feed your fishes. Take a day to rest in your own bed then write up your report." He stood up and ushered her toward the door. "As a thank you for your hard work, I charged your Heartway tokens."

Wrenn looked down at the backs of her hands. She pulled up her sleeves.

Robin had granted her ten Heartway tokens on each arm.

"I don't like those ghosts of yours. They're... ugly." He frowned and waved his hand dismissively. "I want you to stay away from them."

She'd happily stay away from Victor's Heartway ghost, but she would not stop looking for his vampiric monster. Or promise to stay away from Victor's other creation.

She made no response to Robin. No words spoken, or nods given.

No promises. No deals. Her Royal Guard oath meant something to her, even if it meant nothing to him.

Wrenn turned on her heels. She placed her hand on her Royal Guard star as she walked toward the room's grand entrance. She would do her job, no matter how deep the malfeasance in which she swam.

"Don't do anything rash, Wrenn!" Robin called. "You are a Goodfellow!"

She stopped walking, but didn't turn around. "Am I?" she said. *Or am I Victorsdottir?* she thought.

He chuckled. She looked over her shoulder.

Robin pulled out his phone and returned to swiping at the screen. "Remember where your debts lie."

Every one of her cold bones twitched as if restacking themselves. Every nerve and popping joint shifted from attending to its own pain to looking outward at the pain coming.

She'd long wondered if this moment would come. If the fae treachery in which she lived would one day wrap its spindly fingers around her ankles and pull her so deep into its inky depths she no longer saw light.

Because that was the true test. Could she kick hard enough to surface again? Once she resurfaced, would she be able to offer a hand to the others drowning? If not, then why was she a paladin? Why did she wear a Royal Guard star?

Why did she stay with the fae?

Because in her two hundred years, she had done good for everyday fae. She'd solved many other vampire-related cases. She'd helped Rich and Lush several times with miscreants. She'd hauled countless terrible boggarts from the mundane world. She'd done what a lawgiver did.

But this...

She looked up at the rainbows dancing along the practice room's ceiling. This might be a kelpie of a situation looking to make sure she drowned for good.

Robin reached over his shoulder and grabbed something she

hadn't noticed before. "Take this with you," he said.

He'd been carrying Ed's shotgun on his back this entire time? She walked back into the room, hand out, to take the gun.

Robin rotated his hand with the phone so she couldn't see the screen as he held the gun perpendicular to them, with the barrel aimed at the doors and not either of them.

When she wrapped her hand around the stock, he didn't let go. He glanced down at the gun and nodded ever so slightly.

Rainbows danced along every surface of the weapon—rainbows that were not from the refractions in the room, but could easily have been interpreted as such if he hadn't clued her in.

She sighed and took the weapon. "Stealing from mundanes now, are we?" She checked the barrels and unloaded the shells. "Didn't you at least check it first?"

He shrugged and went back to looking at his phone. "Go home," he said, and shooed her away.

Wrenn turned her back on the fae she considered family and walked away.

CHAPTER 29

Wrenn Goodfellow sat at her kitchen table and watched the sunset cast pinks and golds through her sunroom windows. She'd fed her fish and watered her plants. Straightened up, too, and had a light meal when she got home. But mostly, she'd sat at the table staring at the sunroom threshold, waiting.

All of the syndicate-related files except the pixie vellum one were gone when she'd returned home, including her handwritten notes on the pad she'd kept on the table. And she'd logged into her Royal Guard account to find all of her draft reports also missing.

She checked the full Guard database. Her access to files and reports from the Queen's realms had been restricted, which, it seemed, was a "mistake" on the part of the house brownies in charge of IT and would be fixed "shortly."

Wrenn splayed her fingers over the one remaining bit of evidence left to her. The one remaining sheath of pixie vellum that, considering its overall worth, would have been the first thing she would have taken, if she'd been the one sent into a colleague's home to retrieve documents. Because she was pretty damned sure Robin had sent in other Guard to desecrate her home.

So she watched the threshold, waiting. Because her gut said the cutting off of official channels wasn't the only plan the royals had for silencing her.

The sun dropped behind the edge of the window. Dusk flowed into her sunroom all blue and mellow, and settled itself between the plants and the tanks. Her fish blinked. The windows popped a little as they cooled now that the sun no longer warmed their glass. But nothing untold unfolded. No spells manifested.

Victor did not appear.

Wrenn inhaled deeply as if she'd been holding her breath this entire time. The pixie vellum shimmered softly under her hand, and when she picked it up the sweet ballerina once again danced along its edge.

That sprite, the one who'd been sucked dry and tossed into the Titan River, had been a dancer. She'd twirled and pirouetted for the world with her wings fluttering and her magic spiraling around her body like some brilliant cartoon fairy.

She'd been innocence, that one.

Wrenn checked the vellum again. No family, though she did live with a troupe in Applebottom. Wrenn could, at least, give them some closure.

She slid the vellum into its protective sleeve and then into her satchel. And then, on a whim, placed Ed's shotgun in the bag, too. Guns meant nothing in the fae realms. She still wanted it with her in case her place got another visitor while she was out.

She set her Royal Guard star on the table and locked the door behind her.

Lush was serving when she walked into the tavern. They hugged, and Lush thanked her for dealing with the kelpie even if the resulting damage had shut down their kitchen for a good week.

Wrenn took her coffee and made her way down the main street toward her adopted realm's Heartway station. She'd purchased six Robin-free tokens when she left Oberon's Castle. Robin's tokens were on her skin, so they would go with her no matter where she walked, but she still had to at least attempt to be careful.

She dropped a token into her hand. The Heartway should leave her alone, and allow her free passage to Applebottom. She'd offer comfort and generalized handwaving toward justice, and then she'd excuse herself.

There were other vampires out there. Other problems. She'd put her star back on her belt and she'd do her job.

Wrenn dropped her token into the Heartway enchantments, stepped through the shimmer, and... moved.

Dry, furnace-heated air hit her face. Bright midday sun beamed in from massive windows to her left. A multitude of tables, some with their chairs up and some not, surrounded her on all sides.

Across the windows, painted so that it was readable from the outside, were the words "Raven's Gaze is open for delivery and curb-side pick-up."

This was not Applebottom. From the snow and ice outside, she'd landed somewhere in the mundane world.

Alfheim.

"That was easier than I thought it would be."

Wrenn whipped around. A woman she did not know sat alone at a table in the corner. She wore a pristine white t-shirt, a black leather jacket, and black jeans. Her boots looked suspiciously like Wrenn's, as if she'd gotten them off a fae cobbler.

She was not fae, nor was she an elf. Her dark eyes, her lovely straight black hair, and her strong features suggested Native American, but what nation Wrenn didn't know.

She was definitely a magical.

The woman stood and extended her hand. "You are Wrenn Good-fellow, I assume?"

Wrenn gingerly shook the woman's offered hand. "I am. And you are?"

The woman grinned. "Raven," she said.

Wrenn bristled. Raven? *The* Raven? One of the many aspects of Raven? What the hell was going on in Alfheim? "Are you—"

The woman held up her finger. "You have more important business." She pointed out the door as a white truck pulled into the other-wise empty parking lot.

Wrenn walked over to the door and peered outside. "Alfheim Wildcat Sanctuary" blazed across the side of the truck and magic blazed off its driver.

"You're a bit of a peace offering," Raven said. She gently pushed Wrenn toward the door. "Go on. Benta the Nameless has many tales to tell."

The magical named Raven disappeared with a fluttering flourish.

Wrenn sighed. How many times in her two hundred years had she been sidetracked by some magical or another? The Courts especially were always in everyone's business. Seemed Alfheim had the same problem with busybodies.

She pushed open the door and stepped out into the bright sun.

The chill wasn't so bad. The snow snapped and crunched as it melted and the icicles on the tavern's roof dripped in a melodic rhythm.

Two big ravens sat in the big oak tree next to the tavern's walk. They both shimmered in the sun, and when the larger of the two preened its wings, aura sheets of magic filled the tree.

Wrenn waved and both ravens cawed and bobbed their heads in acknowledgement.

Benta stepped out of the truck the moment Wrenn exited the tavern. She closed the driver's door and walked toward Wrenn.

She wore a different jacket than the one she'd had on in the Paul Bunyan Reserve, this one less puffy and a bright, friendly yellow. The hat looked different, too, but still big and wide-brimmed.

She really was extraordinarily beautiful, more beautiful than the Queen with her gray elven eyes, and she moved like the cat in the picture on the side of her truck.

Benta walked up. "I got a call that I was supposed to come pick you up at Raven's Gaze." She pointed at the tavern. "This is Bjorn's place." Her lips scrunched up for a second. "Or was. There's some disagreement right now."

Wrenn pointed over her shoulder. "I met Raven inside," she said.

Benta's lips rounded. "She appeared to you?" She looked impressed. "Raven's been picky about who she'll talk to. Mostly just our Queen and—" She inhaled. "She brought you back here on her own, didn't she? Without asking?"

Wrenn looked back at the restaurant. What was she supposed to say? She'd just been rerouted by the World Raven because she was some sort of "peace offering." There were things happening here she did not understand. "Yes," she said.

"Sorry about that." Benta shook her head. "Anyway, I need to ask you a few questions. Okay?"

Wrenn nodded. "Okay."

"Victor Frankenstein," she said.

"That's not a question," Wrenn said.

Benta chuckled. "Oh, Victor is a huge question, is he not?"

"Was a question," Wrenn said. "He's dead."

Benta nodded. "He died in Edinburgh about two hundred years ago."

"Yes," Wrenn said. "He... lost his head."

Benta chuckled. "How many of your kind are there?"

Wrenn blinked. Benta had to ask that question, didn't she? The one Wrenn didn't know the answer to, not because she didn't know how many of her kind there were, but whether or not she'd been *built*. "Victor resuscitated me," she said. Whispered, really.

Benta's eyebrows knitted. "You're not a witch," she said. "If anything, you're another jotunn."

"I can cast a limited number of spells." She held out her hand to show Benta the spell she used to relocate muscle tension.

Benta sighed. "The magicks you carry are strong and intricate, but I wouldn't expect anything less from Robin Goodfellow. May I?" She reached and drew her finger along the tattoos around Wrenn's wrist. "It'll take some time, but I think we can untangle all of this."

"I carry gifted magic," Wrenn said. "I'm Royal Guard. We all do. But the protection spells are my own."

Benta nodded again. "Oh, honey, you are so much more than Royal Guard."

Wrenn pulled back her hand. "What do you mean?"

Benta nodded toward her truck. "I think it's time you met the other of your kind."

Did she mean Frank? "He..." She inhaled. Ed would not have lied to her. Nor would the elves. Elves don't lie. "The logs and diaries I have said he called himself Adam."

Benta laughed. "*Victor* named him Adam as part of his woe-is-me God complex. When we found him, he didn't have a name."

Neither had Wrenn, when Robin found her. All that time with Victor and he'd only ever referred to her as his pigeon, or his darling, or his love.

Benta ushered her toward the truck. "Come," she said.

Wrenn walked toward the truck, her satchel over her arm and her jitters resurfacing.

She hadn't wanted this. She had work in Applebottom. And she needed time to process what she'd learned from Ed and the elves before coming back to Alfheim.

But it seemed a magical named Raven wanted her here now—and wanted her to meet Victor's other victim.

Because they were both victims, no matter what Victor told her— or the papers Robin had found said. Deep in her bones, she'd always suspected as much. But thinking *he was a monster* had always been easier. Comforting, too, in its own way. The men of Frankenstein were evil, even if one of them had been forced into rage by Victor.

Just like her.

She'd be lying if she said this moment didn't scare her to her core. She wanted to see with her own eyes what to believe.

Benta smiled. "We elves call him Frank."

CHAPTER 30

The hospital, like every other hospital on Earth, wouldn't let the kids in to see their new baby sister. They ran all the normal precautions, too—scanned Ed's temperature on the way in, stuck a rapid-test swab in his nose, scanned him again when he woke up this morning, as directed by the Minnesota Department of Health.

The elves could only do so much when it came to outbreaks.

Grace Maria Martinez made her entrance into the world just as the first rays of morning sunshine crested the horizon—a healthy and hardy babe, one fully blessed by the magicals who considered her their own. The nurses cleaned up mother and child, checked temperatures again, and tucked Ed into the pullout couch in the corner of the room.

He slept for a solid five hours no matter the hospital noise, or the nurses exiting and entering, or little Grace's bassinette moving in and out of the room.

He woke to a darkened room, shades drawn and door closed.

Isabella quietly nursed Grace. "Good afternoon," she said.

Ed stretched his back. Sleeping on a hospital pullout was pretty much like sleeping in the back of a car, complete with leg cramps and lots of beeping.

He stood to stretch his shoulders.

Dagrun Tyrsdottir sat in the chair on the other side of the bed. He hadn't sensed her there, or seen her, or heard her come in. She was mostly out of glamour with her tall elven ears visible and her huge magic ponytail hanging over her shoulder. She was in sweats, though, and wore a pair of grippy hospital socks.

Her arm was still in a cast. Not the same one as the last time he'd seen her, but a larger, longer cast covering her elbow.

She sat ramrod straight, too, like she had a wrap around her ribs.

"Mayor," he said, though when they were out of glamour, etiquette dictated he should refer to her as Queen.

She grinned and nodded toward Isabella and Grace. "She's perfect."

"She is," Isabella said.

"What is your opinion of this Wrenn Goodfellow?" Dagrun asked.

Right to business, that was the Elf Queen of Alfheim.

Ed kissed Isabella's temple. "She latching on okay?" he quietly asked.

Isabella nodded. "Eating like a trooper."

Ed turned his gaze to the elf in the room. "I don't want any more kelpies showing up in Alfheim," he said.

Dagrun gave a small agreeing nod. "None of us do."

"Good," Ed said.

"Any fae of any kind," Dagrun said.

Ed responded with a chuckle. "Your husband made a deal with Queen Titania to get the kids and me out of Texas faster than you all showing up in a plane."

Isabella's eyes widened. "No deals with the fae," she said.

Ed knew exactly what his wife was thinking—he and the kids might be incidental in any deal, but incidental still meant connected. And connected to magicals is what had gotten them here in the first place.

"True," Dagrun said. "Titania isn't the fae we need to be worried about."

Ed pinched his forehead. "Is Remy okay?" He'd forgotten to ask about Gerard and Remy when Arne dropped him off.

"Being in wolfman form gives a fair amount of protection," Dagrun said.

"Yes," Ed said. "I know. But that explosion was magical, caused by a kelpie, and originating from a psychologically messed-up elven sword." Only in Alfheim would Ed use the words *psychologically messed-up* to describe what should have been an inanimate object. "I mean..." He pointed at her broken arm.

Dagrun looked down at the cast. "Remy's healing faster than I am and should be back to his normal self in a few days."

So he'd been correct about the magical severity of the explosion.

"We'll need any information you have on this fae-generated system Wrenn Goodfellow referred to as the Heartway," Dagrun said.

Isabella switched Grace over to her other breast. "That kelpie took my children into whatever this Heartway is."

Dagrun nodded. "It uses ley lines. We had no idea Oberon had upgraded it to the point where it had become the equivalent of a subway system."

"They had no idea Frank lived here," Ed said.

Dagrun shook her head. "This Wrenn person had no idea. I can guarantee you Oberon knew. And that evil..." She looked up at the ceiling. "If the fae were to have an aspect of Loki, his name would be Robin Goodfellow."

"And that's why you're concerned?" Ed asked. They had so *many* things to be concerned about right now.

"Among other things, yes," she said.

Isabella settled Grace in. "We are considering leaving Alfheim," she said. "For the safety of our children."

Dagrun inhaled slowly as if it hurt, then exhaled just as slowly. "We figured as much."

Isabella looked directly at Dagrun. "Tell us why we should stay."

Dagrun leaned back in the chair. "Because Ragnarok is upon us, my friend. And we need your help."

Isabella looked up at Ed with a look he'd seen again and again, not just in his wife's eyes, but in his own. And his parents'. And her parents', too, before they were killed. He knew the look of exhausted resignation that came with moral clarity. The look of someone who would fight to protect everyone's kids, not just their own.

He nodded. "We need to talk about Sophia," he said.

"Yes, we do," Dagrun responded.

"And Wrenn."

"Yes."

Ed kissed Isabella's temple again and walked around the bed. "I can't do my job if I'm not clued in," he said.

"That stops today." Dagrun pointed at a smaller chair in the corner. "Sit down. Please."

Ed grabbed the chair.

"Let's talk."

CHAPTER 31

He went by the name Frank Victorsson. Two hundred years ago, he'd walked out of the Arctic, through Manitoba, and into the part of the world now called Alfheim, Minnesota.

The elves took him in. They gave him a home. Taught him how to channel his Victor-caused anger into becoming a good citizen. He now lived on a beautiful lake outside of town in an equally beautiful cabin-turned-house with none other than the local King and Queen's daughter.

He and Benta used to date.

Not just for a couple of weeks, either. They were on and off for decades. Benta clearly had a lot of ambivalence about the whole thing.

Not that it was any of Wrenn's business.

She sat in the passenger seat of Benta's truck, her satchel on the floor between her feet, leafing through the monthly cat magazine produced by the Alfheim Wildcat Sanctuary. Seemed Minnesota had a couple of sanctuaries specializing in the care of large and small felines of all species. Benta's focus was on rehabbing smaller wildcats like lynxes, bobcats, and a few cougars.

The cats were just as beautiful as the elf.

Wrenn dropped the magazine into the back of the truck. Benta had gone into the house a good twenty minutes ago. Wrenn waited outside while Benta and the other elves in the house argued.

They were just inside the door and probably watching her through the frosted glass. There was movement back there, and a lot of flaring magic.

She was beginning to wonder if Frank Victorsson was even home.

Maybe this was a bad idea. Maybe she should just walk back to Raven's Gaze and ask that aspect of Raven to send her to Applebottom. She'd come back when she felt ready to process all this.

Benta and another elf came out. She was tall like Benta, beautiful too, and in what Wrenn would call a "Mom" glamour.

Benta tapped the window. "Frank's back."

The other elf woman stayed away from the truck. "So you're Frank's sister," she said.

Sister. Did all the elves believe that? Victor was *sure* she and this Frank person would birth a master race.

Or maybe a new kind of mecha-magical.

Wrenn nodded *yes*.

"Sophia and Gabe vouched for you," the other elf said. "We'll be watching anyway."

She wasn't happy, this other elf who was likely Maura, the daughter of the King and Queen. So unhappy about the situation that she refused to introduce herself.

"Okay," Wrenn said.

The one who was probably Maura crossed her arms. "If I catch even a whiff of fae magic I don't like, I'll take off your head. Understand? No warning. No questions. Lennart says you can be trusted but my gut says anyone who calls themselves Goodfellow should have their asses kicked all the way back to the fae realms."

"It's your right to think that," Wrenn said. "I don't blame you." She lifted her satchel off the floor of the truck. She looked between the two elves as she held up the bag. "I have no secret agenda." She didn't. "Ed's shotgun is in here."

Benta took the bag. "And you're telling me this now?"

"Please check it thoroughly before giving it back to him," Wrenn said. "Robin gave it to me."

"What's this?" Benta pulled out the sheath holding the pixie vellum.

How to explain? "I was on my way to talk to the troupe of one of the sprites killed by the kelpies' blood syndicate." She inhaled. "That's the report with the sprite's contact information."

Benta looked at the other elf, then back at the sheath. She tucked it back into the satchel. "Leave the bag."

"That's private information," Wrenn said. "It's a police report."

Benta nodded. "We'll give it back when you leave." She handed the bag to the other woman.

The other elf, the one who was probably Maura, pointed at the gate made from colorful bottles. "Frank's out back."

Wrenn nodded again. Slowly, she opened the door and stepped out of the truck.

"He knows you're here," Benta said.

Wrenn stared at the twinkling rainbow of light refracted through the glass between her and her "sibling." She pointed. "The gate's pretty," she said. Not in the ethereal sprinkling way of the fae, but in a stronger, clearer, more headstrong way.

Like the elves.

Maura snorted.

Benta peered at Wrenn's face. "*Hmmm…*" she said. "You don't need to worry."

Worried? No. Apprehensive, yes.

"Thank you," Wrenn said. Maybe a little worried.

Benta squeezed her hand.

Wrenn nodded again. She squeezed back.

"Good luck," Benta said.

Wrenn walked by Maura and toward the gate. A rainbow of color danced on her skin as she pushed it open, and for a moment, splashed reds and blues across her vision.

Someone had punched the side of the house and cracked the

siding. She picked out small residual magicks in the dent, and along the railing leading up to the deck.

The house wasn't warded, at least not on a level she would have expected.

She stepped up onto the deck.

The entire area between the house and the lake had been set up in three sections stepping down to the water. Each section was its own little living space, the middle one with a covered two-person swing, and one closest to the house had its own large outdoor dining table.

A break in the rail led to a small trail into the trees. Child-created chalk drawings of winged horses covered the planking of the middle section, and several garishly-colored plastic toys were scattered around.

The curtain over the lovely French doors from the house to the deck wavered.

Sophia appeared, along with an elf girl the same age. They pressed their little faces against the window and waved.

Wrenn waved back.

A male elf she sort-of recognized—she was pretty sure he was the other Thor elf—glanced around the curtain. He said something to the girls. The elf girl nodded and waved again, then disappeared. Sophia said something to the elf, then she, too, waved.

Then they disappeared, too.

Wrenn looked around, figuring she would have noticed a man who according to Victor was eight feet tall and terrifying to behold.

The lake lapped at the pebbled shore. Late afternoon sun reflected off the chrome and glass monstrosity of a house on the other side and danced along the water like—

Like Victor, she thought.

That glint only flashed for a second but it screamed blue-white and too bright.

Wrenn scrunched her eyes closed and looked away.

"Are you okay?" a deep, resonant male voice said.

She looked to the side, down the trail that led into the trees.

He stood there, the man who had to be Frank Victorsson. He was huge and wide at the shoulders and more muscular than she'd expected. He wore jeans and a blue jacket with "Gullinbursti Reclamations" embroidered over his left pec. He had on a knit cap much like Ed's too, but this one had some sort of fighting squirrel mascot in the center instead of an Alfheim County Sheriff insignia.

He extended his hand. "Frank," he said as he walked up onto the deck. "You must be Wrenn."

He was classically handsome, with a strong jaw and fiery maroon eyes. A tattoo on the side of his face covered scars, but they weren't even that distracting. The tattoo looked to be Yggdrasil, and shimmered with elven magic.

He wasn't eight feet tall—more likely seven.

Every single one of the exaggerations, the lies, the manipulations Victor had told her were in that foot of difference. Frank Victorsson had a house full of children. Friends, too, and a lot of elven family. This man was not a monster, nor was he brutish and terrifying.

He smiled and jammed his hands into his pockets. "Is this as awkward for you as it is for me?" He looked out at the lake. "Two hundred years and I had no idea you'd survived."

Hands that had a dusting of magic around them. She peered at his shoulders. And there, too, the same dust shimmered in the sunlight.

His face screwed up in a clear indication that he was annoyed by someone or something. "Victor told you I was a monster, didn't he?"

"He told me you tried to drown me to force him to make me your mate."

Frank's face scrunched up into something more angry than annoyed indignation. Wrenn wondered if he realized how easily others could read his emotions.

"I saved that young girl from drowning," he said. "He blamed me for his friend's death. There was a boat." He looked up at the sky. "He told me that I didn't deserve a companion. That I was unlovable and horrific. Then he showed me... parts... that were supposed to be you." He sighed.

"Your mate," she said.

"What?" He looked genuinely confused. "Oh! You see the mate magic, don't you?" He grinned. "Don't worry. It's not for you."

He closed his eyes for a second and when he opened them, he was looking up and to the left. Then the grin turned into the smile of someone in love.

"You look relieved." He leaned a bit toward her as if sharing a secret. "It'd be weird, anyway. It's been two hundred years." He nodded knowingly. "Besides, I've always thought of you as the sister I never had, no matter what Victor thought."

Was she relieved? Happy? Sad? She had no idea.

Out front, Benta's truck started up.

"Benta's leaving?" Wrenn said.

"She's taking Sal in," Frank said. "The elves need her to see if they can crack the fae enchantments on that sword the kelpie left behind. Sal went crazy this morning. Started yelling 'How dare they!' and about how she would 'take care of the fae threat.' We figured it would be best to keep her away from you for now."

"Is Sal another elf?"

Frank laughed. "She's an axe." He scratched at the side of his head. "And a bit possessive."

They stood there for a long moment, neither saying anything. Both watched the lake.

Frank scratched at the tattoo on the side of his face. "Victor Frankenstein had a lot of romantic stupidity in his head. He thought he was entitled to dance along the threshold between the living and the dead." He pointed toward the lake. "He got angry when he came face to face with the consequences of his actions." He sighed. "That anger turned to madness, didn't it?"

She nodded *yes*.

"The only information we found were letters written by a ship captain. We all thought he'd died shortly after I left him on the ice. I didn't learn otherwise until last month." He watched her face for a moment as if trying to read her emotions. "We're not his only creations," he said.

Was she really one of Victor's creations? She was. Did it matter?

"I watched him behead Victor," she said.

His mouth rounded. "I am sorry." He rubbed the top of his hat. "If I'd known, I would have come back." His face said that *coming back* wouldn't have been feasible two hundred years ago. Yet here he was feeling guilty.

"We have a lot to talk about, don't we?" she said.

He motioned her toward the table. "Yes, we do."

They walked toward the house and the seating. He pulled out a chair for her and offered a seat. "Here."

How was it that she'd allowed Victor so much real estate in her head all these years? This man wasn't a monster.

"Thank you," she said.

"You're welcome," he said. "Sister."

Wrenn reached out and took his hand. Why, she didn't know. They'd just met. But for the first time in maybe her entire life, she truly exhaled. She did have family, and not unwanted intrusions into her life from Victor Frankenstein's ghost. "Brother."

The smile he gave her said it all. "Welcome to Alfheim," he said. "Where do we start?"

CHAPTER 32

M r. Frank and Ms. Wrenn were still talking outside in the cold when Mr. Lennart took Gabe and Sophia to their house to get clothes. They were going to stop and pick up dinner at Raven's Gaze, and Gabe was sure Lennart and Bjorn were angry about something to do with the restaurant, but Lennart wasn't particularly specific.

Gabe didn't ask. He'd had enough of magic for a while.

Lennart took a suitcase into Mateo's room and Gabe and Sophia went into theirs. They were to get their homework and any electronics they needed, and at least a week's worth of clothes, just in case. The house was chilly, but not as bad as he thought it was going to be, even though there was a huge hole where the garage should have been. Lennart said Mr. Magnus wanted to build them a mansion, but their Papa had told him then he'd have to build everyone else in Alfheim mansions, too.

Gabe wouldn't put it past the elf to do just that, to make a point.

He rummaged around in his room, got his homework from the family room, packed up his bag, and went to find his sister.

Sophia sat on the floor next to her bed, her bag next to her feet and one of her storage boxes from the closet next to her elbow. She'd tossed all the sweaters that had been in the box onto the bed.

She had a notebook on her lap, one of those leather-bound blank-diary-type books for people who like to journal, except this one looked old.

"What's that?" he asked.

She slammed it shut and tucked it into her bag. "You can't tell Mr. Frank I have his notebook."

She'd stolen a book from Mr. Frank? "Did you take that?" He pushed his way into her room and loomed over her like a babysitter. "Seriously, Sophia! What were you thinking!"

Gabe grabbed it from her bag.

It really was old. The paper inside had dried out and he had to extra careful not to rip anything. "It's blank," he said.

"No, it's not." She grabbed it from his hand.

"Sophia...." Was the notebook magical? He looked over his shoulder at the door. "Does this have anything to do with the kelpie?" Was the book bad?

She thinned her lips. "It's how I knew we were supposed to bring Ranger's bridle home and give it to Mr. Frank."

When Mr. Frank came home this morning, Sophia said she'd handed the bridle to him and told him to take it to someone named Ellie.

Mr. Frank disappeared for a bit after that. Then Wrenn came by.

"I don't like all these magic things we don't understand," he said.

She nodded *yes* as if she, too, felt overwhelmed. "I was really scared of Ranger," she whispered. "And those vampires."

Gabe dropped down to the floor and hugged his sister. He didn't think she'd seen the bodyguard behead his boss, but she had seen the bullets impact his vampire body.

It hadn't been anything at all like gunfire on television. The vampire had popped and snapped and sprayed more than just blood.

"If that notebook is magical," he said. "Mr. Lennart will know."

She shook her head. "The elves think it's useless and no longer magical."

Still, Gabe thought. What if there *was* magic that got by the elves? He didn't want to think about that. Because that meant there might be a way for those vampires to get back into Alfheim.

And the last thing he wanted to think about was vampires.

EPILOGUE

Between The Land of the Living and The Land of the Dead...

He'd been digging so long he'd forgotten who he was supposed to be. No name, no past, no intrinsic understanding of why he slammed the tip of the broken pike into the schist again and again and again.

He only had his work, and Anthea.

She was a lovely vampire, one with bouncy blonde curls, a satisfying plumpness to her hips, and a chatty disposition that filled in his gaps with details about a place called Las Vegas. It was hot and dry but oh so full of life!

He hated deserts. Of all the voids he carried around, those empty spaces that should have been full of memories and wants and desires, he was able to label one: Deserts were good only for invading.

Every so often a little air would leak from that bubble of emptiness called "disdain for deserts" and he'd get a sun-bleached image, or the memory of blowing sand scouring his skin. But then that would stop, and another bubble would fart out the smell of sweet clover, or another would wheeze cliffs and the cold, cold wind over icy seas.

The frightening thing weaving these moments together was not their breadth and variety. It was their synchronicity. Deep down inside him, deep in the blood in his veins, he knew that all of these geographically far-flung memories had happened at the same time.

The same year. The same month. The same exact *moment*.

Such things were not possible.

Yet he dug with Anthea out of a gray place with gray wailing and grayer dust. A place of twilight and vampires.

Such places were also not possible.

Hell was not possible, though he was sure the place from which they sought to escape was not Hell. Just somewhere adjacent. So perhaps he did have an understanding of why he chipped and clanged and stabbed with a pike he knew was a lot more than the dead piece of gray metal.

Magic, it whispered. Or not. Perhaps the whispering came from the blood—*bloods*—pumped by his (vicious) heart.

Vicious, it whispered.

He stopped for a moment, pike in his inordinately large hand, his shoulder sore under the bleak, dead armor he wore. Why did his shoulder hurt? Why would he think of his armor as dead?

Magic.

Anthea looked up at him with her preternatural violet eyes. He was almost twice her height. Not quite, more or less a yard or a meter or... He did not remember his measurements. There were many, and most were not synchronous.

She was Anthea of Las Vegas, that place of dry and hot, but the black dress she wore was something wholly different.

It flickered out around her, blackness more black than the absence of light, yet all the illumination in their pit came from the dress's shimmering obsidian sheen and its crow-feather-like refracted rainbows.

It was the absorption of all colors at the same time it reflected back darkness.

And it had a mind of its own. It made him uneasy even though he should have made her—and it—quake in their boots.

She smiled and stretched up onto her toes to touch his cheek.

"This is how I become a valkyrie," she said. Then she and the dress returned to digging.

So they dug, and dug, and dug.

The hole was now so deep they couldn't climb out. Anthea chattered on about her kingdom of Las Vegas, with its glowing lights and loud noises. About expensive chariots and dancing women and mundane magicians who specialized in all sorts of slight-of-hand.

Her chattering occasionally triggered his mind to make shapes and places out of the shadows in their pit, and sometimes those shapes and places triggered other, strange, asynchronous memories.

He'd dug himself out of a prison, once. Not for the time he chased down a maiden in a dark forest, and not for any similar crime. He could not remember why, yet there had been mortar between cut bricks of granite, and the constant drone of the sea outside. Seagulls and the smell of dead turtles had wafted up from the beach.

And every so often, he'd remember names. A place called Castilla. Tribunals and God and Queens and Kings. Pain and anguish and begging for the release of death.

Then more digging.

And one day, the floor of their pit became the wall of their tunnel. They both felt a pull, a need to dig *up*, and turned accordingly.

Neither he, nor Anthea, nor the dress understood how long it took for the turn to block the dust and howling from the Hell-adjacent territory behind them. Time and space meant nothing here, nor did hunger, or yearning, or pain. They were inside the structures between life and death and they burrowed between day and night. Between fire and ice. They bathed in the frozen ashes of murdered worlds.

They dug upward, chipping at the limestone, breaking through new layers of schist.

Finally hitting dirt.

They'd found the edge of The Land of the Living—the dark place where the boundary became more life than death. Where living things worked in the service of death. The soft place filled with bugs and beetles and worms.

Anthea chattered about how this could not be Las Vegas because the loam here was too rich and hearty. The soil smelled fresh, not like a desert, and clearly had been tended lovingly by whomever tilled here.

Perhaps they had found the land she sought—the place where she could fulfill her destiny to become a thing called a valkyrie.

"This might not be the world you remember," he said. They were as likely to break through into another circle of Hell as they were to find the place they'd called home.

She shrugged and her soft blonde curls bounced sweetly around her rosy apple cheeks. "But it *is*, my love," she said.

She'd begun calling him "my love" what felt like centuries ago. Strangely, it satisfied a craving he did not realize he had. Or, more accurately, a hunger that up until now had never been sated.

He did not argue. How could he argue with the round, blonde vampire whose touch fulfilled all his small hungers?

He hit the ceiling of their tunnel and the tip of the pike broke into air.

Sweet air. Fresh air. Cold air.

Snow drifted down through the hole.

"Oh!" Anthea said. "This is definitely not Las Vegas!" She jumped to get a better look. "Lift me up, love," she said as the dress flowed over her hand. "Gloves, you know."

He lifted her up so she could peer through the hole. She grinned.

Then she stuck her fingers through and into the air.

"Is it night?" he asked. She wasn't a vampire who could walk in daylight. He probably wasn't either, though he couldn't remember that any more than he could remember his name.

She pulled back her hand. "It is!" She kissed his dusty forehead. "We're home!"

He set her down and peered up at the hole. More snow dusted his face. He shook it from his eyes and laughed.

Parts of him remembered snow. Scandinavian fjord snow. Ural snow. Flakes dropping through Black Forest trees. Snows high up in the Pyrenees.

All the snows from all the times and the places.

He blinked and rubbed his cheek. These flashes would be his undoing.

A few more pokes with the head of the pike and the roof of their tunnel collapsed. Fresh air flowed in and moonlight laid down a beautiful, clean, silver sheen.

Anthea laughed and clapped her hands. And the dress...

The dress inhaled the world above and exhaled out all their burrowing dust. The shimmers that had been muted obsidian became gleaming black glass. The reflections that had been covered with dirt now danced with the refractions of crow feathers.

The dress wasn't alive. Not in the living way of bugs and beetles, or birds and bats. It responded, and it processed, and it did what it wanted, but it was something more than life. Or something less. It was a force all by itself.

And it wanted back into the mundane world even more than he did.

He lifted Anthea up far enough that she could pull herself through the hole. He attached the pike to the harness on his back that he'd fashioned from his armor's plating. Then he dusted his hands and gripped the edges of the hole.

The giant who did not remember his name, the huge man with the bolt scar on the side of his face and the inert magical armor on his body, pulled himself back into the world of people.

Anthea sat on a rock only a few paces away. She stared out over a lake as a halo of blonde curls surrounded by wave after wave of all the types of blackness.

She looked over her shoulder and smiled. "There you are," she said.

"How long have you been waiting?" he asked.

She shrugged again. "An hour. Maybe a bit more."

And yet their pit had strung time along like his synchronous and asynchronous mind.

She tilted her head as she often did when she read his thoughts from the pulls and pushes of his face. "We moved through a veil," she said, as if that was enough to explain the strangeness of the missing hour, maybe a bit more.

She stood and flowed toward him. "We were chosen, remember? The dress wants us to do good now."

She'd spoken many times about being a "bad" capable of "good" and that's why the dress chose her. Why all the dresses chose who they chose.

But he was not the wearer of a dress. He was just an eight-foot man with a broken pike and no memory of why he had hungers.

The dress fed them somehow, but they were still there, powerful and deep down in his bloods. Strong. Every single soul whipping around inside his chest wanted to feed, except for him.

He rubbed his ear. He confused himself as much as Anthea confused him about "kingdoms" and "power" and there always being a kernel of good. *Always.* Otherwise there wasn't a circuit to exchange energy. And without the circuit, and the exchange, there was no life.

That's how all the magicals came about, she'd said. That kernel called out and power rubbed up against power. Sparks followed, and energy flowed. And then the chaotic destruction of the universe coiled itself up into something that gave enough of a damn to regulate the flow.

Thus began what Anthea called the Universals: Turbulence, Injection, Deletion, and Entropy.

He walked over to her rock. A thin layer of ice had formed over most of the lake and reflected the volcano at the end of the valley.

She pointed at the lake. "This is not the land of the valkyries."

He'd seen images of that mountain before, of its snow-capped symmetrical cone and its steep sides. Of the plateau of clouds that formed around her peak. Of the valley that now framed the view.

"Where are we?" he asked. He remembered images drawn on rice paper traded from faraway lands, and later photographs. Silk armor, too, and swords so sharp they severed limbs with ease.

"I think that's Mount Fuji," Anthea said.

Were they in... Japan? *Nippon*, he thought.

Her eyes widened and she pressed up against his side. "There are oni here," she breathed. "Oni who have taken the attributes of vampires."

She pointed.

The fox sat on the shore of the lake grooming the black tips of her ears as if she were a cat. She wiggled her fox snout. Then she stretched forward and shook her red fur from her head to her tails.

One, he thought, as he watched. And then it was three. Then seven.

And when she stretched her back legs and shifted her body forward, her front legs becoming arms and her head becoming human, he counted nine.

Then she became a radiant woman, beautiful beyond words with the silkiest, blackest hair and perfect porcelain skin. She dressed in flowing traditional robes in primary colors, in patterns that screamed *imperial*.

He blinked. Anthea inhaled.

The kitsune stood directly in front of them.

"Well, *well*," she said. "*What* do we have *here?*" She cocked her head to the side at a painful angle and poked him in the chest. "Is that a *dragon* I see on your armor, my dear huge warrior?"

He looked down at the crest on his dull and lifeless armor. "Perhaps," he said. The insignia was stylized, so he did not know for sure what it represented. A dragon was certainly possible.

The kitsune clapped once. "It *is!*"

Anthea looked up at his face, then at the kitsune, then back up at him. She opened her mouth, but then pinched her lips shut.

The kitsune grabbed Anthea's jaw. "This gift." She swirled her hand near the dress. "Is precious beyond all the magic in the world, my Lord!" She laughed. "We thank you!"

She stuck her fist into the blackness of the dress.

"Do not touch!" Anthea screamed.

"Why?" the kitsune said. "You are the sacrifice here, are you not? The gift to those from whom the Master of Vampires would demand tribute?" She reached for the dress again. "He knows the truth. I am a more worthy host."

The dress recoiled and ballooned out like a sail to keep the kitsune from touching it.

The kitsune frowned. Her nostrils flared and she waved her hand at the wider world. "Why do you fret so? Your sibling has been *busy* with the mundanes, has it not? So, so busy." She *tsked*. "Do *you* not wish to ride again?"

"You have *no idea* what I am," Anthea said. She blinked as if suddenly aware that she hadn't said the words that had come out of her mouth.

The kitsune shrugged dismissively. "Is that so?" She laughed melodically as if Anthea had said the silliest thing. "You are four. That is all that matters."

"Leave her alone," he said. This creature made his skin crawl as if that part of him who remembered the prison, and the sun, and the fresh sea air understood what it was looking at.

The kitsune covered her mouth with the tips of her fingers as if to stifle a giggle. "Come now. You must be *famished*. I am." She cocked her head to the side again, kissed those fingers, and reached out as if to set that kiss on his lips.

He grabbed her wrist. "How dare you touch me, minuscule worthless fox," he growled. But he hadn't said those words any more than Anthea had said *You have no idea what I am*.

She'd been correct; he had no idea who he was. *What* he was. How he carried so much magic—he felt it coiling around his body, and Anthea's, and this horrid little vermin's. But this part of him in control —the part that responded to the world so mundanely—it couldn't access that magic.

But *he* could.

"I have a brother." He remembered a bolt of lightning. Old magic, and a fool named Victor Frankenstein. And a... bride. A woman.

He looked up at the moon as it gleamed off the shoulder of Mount Fuji. This land was a paradise mundanes did not deserve.

Nor did the kami and their yoked demons.

The armor once manifested by the most willful of his parts lifted off his skin. It puffed into its constituent ash like a shroud of visible magic. Then it settled back onto his shoulders as the exquisitely tailored suit he preferred.

The pike, though, would need extra care. For now, it remained broken and on his back.

Anthea gasped. "We need to leave," she said, but not to him, or to the kitsune. She said it to the dress.

"Go," he said. He'd give her this boon. It was she, after all, who had drawn this snack to him. For a moment, he thought of sharing his spoils, but thought better of it. Anthea was not a vampire who would respond well to carrying the power of such a kitsune in her blood.

The dress coiled around Anthea's plump body and up into her blonde curls. The kitsune hissed.

Anthea and the dress vanished.

"The Emperor will *not* be happy," the kitsune snarled.

She fidgeted and shook and clearly did not understand the threat he posed. Which seemed interesting, since she was the most magical of kitsunes. And so, so naughty.

"Whatever," Brother said. He snapped his fingers. "Where are my manners? My last turn was in the States." He adjusted his cuffs. "Tell me, is there a Japanese equivalent to an irreverent American eye roll?"

The kitsune hissed.

No, she had no idea who was now in charge of his body.

"Dear Anthea was correct. You have no idea what you let into your beautiful country." He snatched the kitsune around the neck and lifted her into the air.

She spit in his eye.

Brother chuckled. "No idea at all."

How long had it been since he'd felt the satisfying pressure in his jaw as his fangs extended? Or the sating flow of warm, rich blood over his tongue? He slammed his mouth against the kitsune's neck. And the taste of such magic and power!

He dropped the fox's hollow corpse onto the frozen shore of a pristine Japanese lake. Slowly, carefully, he ran a finger around his lips. Best not to waste a drop of something so precious as the blood of a nine-tailed kitsune.

Why let his parts fight each other? Why settle for simply being the original vampire, the King of a long-dead Eastern European hovel and the pretender to the world's throne, when he could be more than the sum of his parts?

He understood now the old magic in his blood that made his memories synchronous and asynchronous, current and serial, local and global. Why he had allowed that dress—and he knew exactly what that dress was, and what she meant for the world—to be the bait needed to draw in the worst, tastiest monsters of this lovely island.

He squatted next to the kitsune's body. Such moments required reverence. "I thank you, my dear," he said. Then he stood and rolled his shoulders.

He had not been a part of this world's events for ... how long? He gazed at the moon. "I do believe we are still some time from Samhain," he muttered. So, a week, perhaps. Now he had returned, fully capable and flush with such *power*. This island truly was a paradise.

Where else would a god make his new home?

GOD FORSAKEN

When Lollipop comes looking to call in Frank's debts, Frank and Wrenn find themselves in Tokyo and embroiled in a Frankenstein family reunion neither of them wanted—nor thought possible.

The Vampire God formerly known as Brother has escaped his prison. Add angry kami, needy mate magic, a language neither Frank nor Wrenn understands, fragile international magical diplomacy, and… well, culture really can be a shock.

GOD FORSAKEN, Northern Creatures #7, available June 10th!

GET FREE BOOKS

SUBSCRIBE TO KRIS AUSTEN RADCLIFFE'S NEWSLETTER

You will be notified when Kris Austen Radcliffe's next novel is released, as well as gain access to an occasional free bit of author-produced goodness. Your email address will never be shared and you can unsubscribe at any time.

WWW.SIXTALONSIGN.COM/MAILING-LIST-SIGN-UP/

THE WORLDS OF
KRIS AUSTEN RADCLIFFE

Smart Urban Fantasy:

Northern Creatures

Monster Born

Vampire Cursed

Elf Raised

Wolf Hunted

Fae Touched

Death Kissed

God Forsaken

Magic Scorned

Witch Burned (*coming soon*)

*Genre-bending Science Fiction about
love, family, and dragons:*

WORLD ON FIRE

Series one

Fate Fire Shifter Dragon

Games of Fate

Flux of Skin

Fifth of Blood

Bonds Broken & Silent

All But Human

Men and Beasts

The Burning World

Dragon's Fate and Other Stories

Series Two

Witch of the Midnight Blade

Witch of the Midnight Blade Part One

Witch of the Midnight Blade Part Two

Witch of the Midnight Blade Part Three

Witch of the Midnight Blade: The Complete Series

Series Three

World on Fire

Call of the Dragonslayer (*coming soon*)

Hot Contemporary Romance:

The Quidell Brothers

Thomas's Muse

Daniel's Fire

Robert's Soul

Thomas's Need

Quidell Brothers Box Set

Includes:

Thomas's Muse

Daniel's Fire

Roberts's Soul

ABOUT THE AUTHOR

Kris's Science Fiction universe, **World on Fire**, brings her descriptive touch to the fantastic. Her Urban Fantasy series, **Northern Creatures**, sets her magic free. She's traversed many storytelling worlds including dabbles in film and comic books, spent time as a talent agent and a textbook photo coordinator, as well written nonfiction. But she craved narrative and richly-textured worlds—and unexpected, true love.

Kris lives in Minnesota with one husband, two daughters, and three cats.

For more information
www.krisaustenradcliffe.com

www.ingramcontent.com/pod-product-compliance
Lightning Source LLC
Chambersburg PA
CBHW060431180626
46817CB00007B/2760